About the Author

Born, brought up and educated in London, the author is happily married and now lives in Surrey. Following a successful career, she has now turned back to an early ambition to write a novel, not having had time whilst earning a living.

A One-Man Woman?

T. J. Thomas

A One-Man Woman?

Olympia Publishers
London

www.olympiapublishers.com
OLYMPIA PAPERBACK EDITION

A CIP catalogue record for this title is
available from the British Library.

ISBN: 978-1-80074-143-0

This is a work of fiction.
Names, characters, places and incidents originate from the writer's
imagination. Any resemblance to actual persons, living or dead, is
purely coincidental.

First Published in 2021

Olympia Publishers
Tallis House
2 Tallis Street
London
EC4Y 0AB

Printed in Great Britain

Dedication

To the current one man in my life, my husband

Acknowledgements

To all the friends who help each other, share their problems and give support.

A must read for anyone who has a loved one cheating on them and/or the third party.

-A friend who was helped.

PART ONE
NOW

Chapter 1
Leaving

He had gone. One minute I was numb inside and out, the next minute I wanted to tear my insides out. How can you make yourself not care for someone you love? If all the hurt I had been caused could not do it, would I have to wait until I died, or perhaps even bring on my own death? There were minutes I felt like stabbing myself through the heart to ease the pain, but deep inside I knew I was too strong and worth too much for that. I could not do it to others who would be affected, family that I loved in a different way. I had always been taught that blood was thicker than water; family meant a lot to me. Funnily enough, I always knew my father was right. He was wrong about a lot of things he said and did, but not in the things he taught me about people and life. I wish he could have taught him more as well; I believe he tried for me; they became such good friends. So much seemed to be going on in my head and thoughts, I could not focus on any one thing.

Tomorrow would be three weeks after my forty-first birthday and two days after Christmas day. Life begins at forty so they say. I could not believe my life had begun last year, so for me that saying does not hold true. But then again, I had listened to one of the radio forethoughts for the day that week on which they advocated that all ends are new beginnings; the death of someone holds a new start for those left behind. This feels worse than if he had died, so maybe.

What had he said, so many things, repeatedly, since that birthday? I still was not sure we had done the right thing by waiting until both our families had been to our home for Christmas day, but it is done now. It was not the best of Christmas days, in fact the worst, but I think they were all glad they came and enjoyed it. We concealed it all well, I wonder what I will tell them and when. I wonder why it matters so much to me. Can some people just care too much and drive others away? He said he felt trapped, but I had never been clinging or restrictive. I had only wanted what he wanted to give me, and I gave him all my love, unconditionally. Perhaps he gave too much at the outset and that is why I missed it so much when he stopped. I had suppressed my feeling and emotions from people around me for as long as I can remember. He saw more of my feelings than anyone else; perhaps I should have let him see it all. I just do not know, maybe I never will. Is there any chance we could ever be 'us' again?

At least my ambition as a little girl to go to the Ritz had been achieved. Not quite the breakfast at the Ritz I had dreamed about and imagined him taking me to. A glass of dry white wine on my forty-first birthday was better than never seeing inside, even if it did end in despair.

It had a funny side I suppose, looking back if we forgot about the few days before. He had been to the Ritz a number of times with his mates so I was surprised when he looked a bit uneasy, but we sat down in the bar and I made my usual wasted and unnoticed efforts to help him relax. He ordered wine for me and an orange juice for himself, which was unusual. Some peanuts and olives came first, and we were both quite hungry and had not yet decided where to eat, a treat for my birthday. We indelicately scoffed the lot. My glass arrived with lipstick on it and being my false assertive self, I apologised for asking for it to be changed. I had a fresh glass and enjoyed being there and drinking it with him. I always had a tendency to watch other people in bars and restaurants, and that night I watched a couple get annoyed with the woman who was with them, a mother or mother-in-law, obviously widowed, getting drunk on sherry and speaking louder and louder, to their embarrassment. James got annoyed at me for even noticing when I pulled a face and commented on it. I was hungry and sad so when he offered me another drink, I said no thanks. He shrugged as if I had done the wrong thing again, and asked for the bill. It was ages coming and understandably he got irritated again. He finally paid the excessive price for two drinks, picked my coat up to help me on with it and promptly knocked my glass across the room to smash in tiny pieces on the floor. How embarrassing. I think I apologised and tried to ignore it, the waiter said not to worry, and it was not mentioned again as we slowly walked out. I remember when we would have giggled together over something like that. Now, one of us would just attempt to change the subject when things went wrong, usually me. At this point in time, we had one subject that kept cropping up between us. I could not stop pushing it until I found out the truth.

We had been under such pressure all day; I sometimes wonder how I did not totally crack up with the mental and emotional pressures I had borne. I am sure others have stood up to worse, but many have gone through much less and not survived. On the way to the restaurant the tears came but still not the truth, that took another week. We did not make the restaurant; we went home after I burst into tears. I apologised again and cooked a simple meal, well not exactly, I heated up something frozen and drank another glass of wine on my own. He said he did not want one. I remembered all the bottles we had shared and me jokingly complaining he drank most of it. Maybe we would share one on New Year's Eve; he said he wanted to spend it with me. Having Scottish grandparents and a close family, New Year's Eve was always incredibly significant to me. It meant more than Christmas and birthdays, perhaps not as much as our anniversary.

Early next year we will have been married twenty years. I cannot believe this is happening. I would have known before now if we had got 'us' wrong. I do not yet know the whole truth. I should know enough to be glad to see the back of him, but all I can think of is us being happily together again because we both want it. Am I kidding myself there is even a chance? Does he have any love left for me?

Look on it as a break, sit back and reflect, let us see how we feel, give it time. I feel trapped; I need the freedom to do what I want. I want to see what life is like not being married. I am forty-one years old; I might have another fifty years on this planet. He repeated those statements many times to convince me or himself, or both, I am not sure. I have got these needs. I have got to get it out of my system, maybe it will bring us together again. It is about me. I have got these needs. If it is over, we have got to face up to it, we can still be friends. I am not going out of your life forever. I feebly mentioned my needs, but they did not seem to come into it. I finally told him I did not need him, I did not want him, did not need, or want, anybody. I always had and always would look after myself. I thought it was what he wanted to hear; it certainly was not the truth. It probably sounded to him like one of my, what he would call, throw away lines. Will it ever come back? It was, and still is, one of those special rare loves that so many people search for and never find. Nothing is ever perfect, but I know it is too much to give up on. If my love is no longer wanted, what then? I genuinely believe his life is better for having my love and always will be, and I care enough, even after everything, to want only ever to give my life and love to him. Perhaps that is what made him feel trapped. Should I be trying to stop my feelings for him which have grown so deep, it feels like a cancer I cannot stop, it is tearing at my insides like a twelve bladed knife turning and turning?

"Use the time to reflect," he said, "And see how you feel." I felt as if part of me was no longer there; it had been taken away or destroyed, I was not sure which. We were both seventeen when we met, children he says now, although we did not think that at the time.

Chapter 2
France

A few weeks earlier, one Saturday morning, I had been dithering for about a week. I knew I needed some space to think and I had some leave due at work. I picked up the phone and rang the airline. Credit card number quoted, and my ticket was on the way. "I did not think you would go," he said, looking pleased.

"I know," I said.

"It will be good for you," he said.

I replied, "You could still come with me if you wanted." He said he did not have enough leave, a lie. Despite my trepidation and doubts, I was really pleased when the ticket came. I had done it, I even arranged for car hire at the airport for me. It was expensive but I did not fancy travelling from the airport to the house alone. I was not sure of train times or routes or taxi availability. We had bought an old village house in France as an investment four years ago and went together from time to time, but always drove from England.

He did not take me to the airport, although he offered in a way you do not accept; I knew he did not want to. I also thought it unfair as he had to get to work. Anyway, I wanted to be independent. On the train to the airport I said to myself you have done it now, enjoy it, relax, it will give you time to think. I said maybe he will miss you so much that when you meet again, the passion and love will return. Perhaps an old welcoming kiss and into bed and make love.

I arrived at Gatwick much too early and rang him at the office to say I had arrived as he asked me to. I did not want him to think I needed to keep ringing him, so I intended to keep any calls to a minimum. He was not in his office, so I left a message to say I had rung. The flight went well after a delayed start. I had the usual minimal conversation with fellow passengers, but did not over respond as I did not want to keep it going. I telephoned from the airport to say I had arrived, and he seemed pleased to hear from me and asked me to let him know when I arrived at the house. It felt like he wanted to track me and make sure I was there. I picked the car up and got used to it with the left-hand drive quite quickly. I was a bit nervous driving alone but felt okay, until I took a wrong turn. I laughed at myself. It was a joke between us when we went wrong, of it being James' fault when he was driving and when he was map reading, never mine. I then felt lonely.

The house was cold, dirty, and damp when I arrived. As it was dark, I was afraid to air it because of mosquitoes and other insects getting in. It was so lonely without him, but I forced myself into making the bed and getting some food for the evening from the village. The leak from the roof terrace, which we knew about from the previous visit, was nowhere near as bad as I had expected and feared, so when I went to telephone him, I told him it did not look bad but I would have a better look in daylight next day. He did not show any concern for me coping with it. I sat and read my book that evening. It was one of those that make you cry; I am not sure it was only the book but that is what I put it down to. I did not sleep well but got up brightly next morning and cleaned the house. Perhaps my standards are too high, but I did not think much of the people who had left it closed for the winter for us. They were people James knew from work and I did not. There were breadcrumbs around and dirty dustbins, and a general unclean state everywhere. I was glad I had come in that respect and not left it for a few more months after their visit. It would probably have been infested with something. So, straight away I felt I should have come even if for the wrong reason. The terrace had obviously leaked and stained the ceiling and wall, but I had been told that the storms recently had been extreme. It was raining that day and only a tiny trickle of water appeared. I did not think it was a great cause for concern but did not know much about roofs and leaks. Once the house was cleaned and aired it did not feel so damp and dismal, but it was not a cheerful environment.

I decided to go to the nearest town for some shopping and a look at the beautiful lake close by. It stopped raining for me as I arrived at the lake, and I got out of the car and walked as far as I could, just thinking about James being with me. I was not sad at being alone, just remembering the happiness we had shared. I had such happy memories of the first occasion we had been there, and the last one when we went wind surfing. Then, I suddenly remembered that had not been such a happy time. He had done this before and hurt me badly.

I did not want to drink much but wanted to spoil myself, so I bought some small bottles of Kriter, one a night. I did not have the confidence to eat out alone in France at that time of year when all is quiet, so I bought a chicken to cook which would last me the whole of my stay. I again rang him that afternoon, only because he had asked me to. I told him what I had been doing. He did not sound too interested or too bright.

He said he was off to a meeting that evening and he asked me to ring him in the morning, Saturday. He seemed to want to hear from me, which made me hope he was missing me, but he did not say so.

I was up early and desperate to talk to him but did not want to wake James, so I waited until nine a.m.; no reply. Stupidly, I felt so empty but forced myself out for the day. It was raining again so I went to another town to look at the shops and I rang him again. He said he had been out for a run when I rang earlier, and he sounded happy to hear from me, and was cheerful and talkative. I could not work out his mood changes. That lonely, empty feeling came back when we hung up; he had told me he was going to a football match and wanted me to call again that evening between five and six o'clock.

The weather changed so I left the town and went to the beach; it was lovely and almost deserted. I walked along the pier and a couple of fishermen looked at me but did not speak. I sat and ate my lunch and read my book, and felt at ease and rested, and was really enjoying it. Then a cyclist came along and sat a few feet away from me giving me the usual pick up looks, which just made me feel uncomfortable. I was not looking for anything like that; maybe I should have been, so I went for a walk along the beach. It can only happen to me, a huge stray dog started following me. It seemed to want to play but warnings of rabies had never drawn me towards French dogs. I ignored him, but it started running in circles and charging towards me and jumping up. I was terrified and slowly left the beach. As I did, another dog came along and he preferred him to me. James would laugh at me, I thought. I finally braved it and went in a bar for a drink alone. It was quiet; I had seen another woman go in on her own, but she turned out to be a friend of the barman. Anyway, I had a coffee and used the toilet and it was not so bad. I headed back to the house with my mind only on speaking to James again. He said he had enjoyed the football and did not know what he would do with his evening. He did not sound very bright again and said he would probably go for a pizza.

I rang again early next morning as he had asked me to, but there was no reply. I tried a couple more times in case he had gone for a run again, but no reply. It was dry and sunny that day, so I wrapped up and went to a different beach. I had a drive around our usual haunts and found places we had not been before, and was eager to tell James about them. I walked along paths, the cliffs and beaches, and tried him on every phone box I passed but could not get a reply. I sat on the beach in a sheltered and isolated spot and just relaxed, looking at the view, reading my book. I even had a quick paddle, but it was icy cold. I heard a car door slam, and a while later a man came walking past me, closer than necessary. I ignored him; I suppose a lot of women would have enjoyed the attention, but I did not and felt uncomfortable. He waited around a bit and said something I did not quite catch as he left. Half an hour later, a couple of men with a little girl walked past and met someone they knew just in front of me. They chatted for ages and I tried to listen to what they said, not nosy just wanted to improve my French. It was to do with buying and selling a boat. Every time I looked in their direction, one of the men caught my eye. He was enjoying it; he had a mischievous glint in his eye that says do you want to get to know me. I did not respond, and they eventually left. I had the beach to myself and despite the chill wind in my sheltered spot, the sun was lovely and warm on my face. I felt more relaxed than I had in a long time and just hoped I could take it back with me to share with James. I forced myself not to ring him until later as I guessed he must have gone out for the day. Deep inside, I felt something was wrong.

The man who had been on the beach earlier, returned and walked purposefully towards me. As he opened his mouth to speak, I stood up and picked up my things and walked away. He followed me off the beach and watched me get into my car. I am so cautious with people like that. I locked myself in and drove off. He got in his car and appeared to follow me; my legs were shaking, and I was very afraid. I jumped two sets of traffic lights and took a turning I did not want, to lose him, which luckily I did. I wondered if I was neurotic or sensible. I will never know. I had been a married woman for a long time and out of touch with how you are picked up.

I left it as late as I could that evening to ring James. It was not very pleasant walking to the phone box in the dark village. He told me he had been to Brighton for the day, looked around the harbour, and sat and read. I had that deep inner feeling, listening to him, that something was wrong again. He told me he had missed me. I said how crazy it was that we were both on the beach reading, about a thousand miles apart.

Those inner feelings plagued me a bit the next day, but I talked myself out of being ruled by my imagination and brightened myself up with the fact that I would be seeing him the next day. How much I was looking forward to it, it was such an indescribable feeling. I felt relaxed still. I had spent the evening grouting the tiled floor and I worked late finishing it as I wanted it to be a surprise for him when we next came together, so I made up my mind not to tell him I had done it.

I left early next day. I wanted to buy him a present,

something French, from Montpelier, before I got the plane. For some reason, a terrible pain came in my side and my period started, which upset me because of how I hoped we would make love when I got back. I had forced myself not to think negatively about us while I was away and I did not want to start now, so I thought well by the weekend I should still feel good and my period would be over. I forced my other feelings away.

After many shops and feeling tired I found exactly the present I wanted, a Pierre Cardin scarf in grey cashmere which I really loved. The price was ridiculous but as I purchased it, I was full of love and the need to give it to him.

I rang him from the airport, and he had decided to meet me at Victoria; he said he had a meeting that night he particularly wanted to go to. He agreed to wait until seven o'clock; if the plane was delayed and if I was later than that, I would get a taxi. The trip back was like the outward journey apart from more persistent chatter in the next seat. I responded but my mind was elsewhere. I wanted to be at Victoria on time, so I ran from the plane to the Tube with my case and bags. I wished so much the pain in my side would go away. I think I was worried as to the cause as well. Maybe just stress.

He was waiting at the end of the platform. My heart opened when I saw him as it always did when we met after a break. He genuinely seemed pleased to see me. We chatted briefly and drove to his meeting and dropped him off. I drove myself home and unpacked; it was not the same as if he had come with me, but I could unwind and wait for him. The uneasy feeling came back when he looked me in the eye later. I did not want to spoil things because of my imagination, so I gave him his present and told him all about my trip. Things seemed okay until I asked him about what he had done which led to his day in Brighton. I just knew, one hundred percent, that there was more to it than a day in Brighton. I went back to work next day, Wednesday. The pain was still there at the weekend, but it had improved enough that I convinced myself I need not go to the doctor. I did not mention it to him.

The weekend passed so quickly as usual; the Christmas shopping had to be started. I knew he did not like Christmas, I still do not know why. We both had presentations to give at work that week. We were both the types that this put us under a lot of strain and pressure. We practised on each other and it helped us both. We did not make love that weekend. My presentation was in Edinburgh on Thursday and Friday. His was in London on Thursday. We both had responsible jobs.

Chapter 3
Edinburgh

James dropped me off at the office in his Porsche on Wednesday morning; we wished each other luck with our awesome tasks and kissed goodbye. My trip started off badly; we allowed an hour and a quarter to get from the office to Heathrow and get on the plane to Edinburgh. For some reason, it took ages on the Tube; I got body searched and my luggage was searched, and we missed the plane by one minute. We had two hours to kill; my colleague, Tony, and I chatted mainly about work and our training course for the next two days. We seemed to get on well; we had not worked together very much before. I was not uptight or struggling to find things to say. I wanted to try and enjoy the trip and the course. I had practised and knew my subjects. For some reason, I wanted to do it particularly well without too many signs of nerves. We spent that afternoon in the Edinburgh office discussing the programme with the Scottish manager. I started to feel my nerves when I realised, I kept telling people it was the first time I had used a slide projector in a live environment. I had been given instructions on the presentation skills course I had attended but that had been ages ago in preparation of another presentation. When I had come to use what I had learnt, the bulb blew and we had to sit around a table looking at my slides. Luckily, it had been an informal environment, but it was on my mind and this was to be my debut. It was quite stressful.

That evening we booked into our hotel, which was unexpectedly very pleasant and reasonably priced. Tony and I went to our rooms and agreed to meet in the bar before dinner. I was first, but determined not to appear shy or embarrassed alone, I ordered a tomato juice. I could have done with something stronger but was thinking of the next day. The waiter offered me the menu, but I said there would be two of us and, as a result, felt a lot better. Tony was not long in arriving and I bought him a beer. We chatted and both agreed we did not want a late night as we both wanted to read our notes. We had a pleasant meal and talked together in a relaxed way about people at work, ourselves, life, politics; we even touched on Ireland, which is a subject I usually avoid. We did have a bottle of wine, which Tony put on his bill. I made a mental note to pay my way next day. I fancied a Perrier after, so we had a quick drink in the bar before turning in. I rang James from my room and he was home, having just returned, he said, from playing squash at his office social club. He did not sound very cheerful again and I assumed he was nervous over his presentation next day. I certainly was. I tried to put a bright voice on even though I felt low at the tone of his. We wished each other luck and agreed to let the other know how things went next day.

The course participants were extremely friendly, which certainly helped me. The first two sessions were covered by three speakers from Scotland, two of whom were obviously extremely nervous. The female was so bad she was covered in red blotches and sweaty, but nevertheless gave her presentation reasonably well. I really felt for her as I had been like that myself on previous occasions and partially suspected

I would be again, but seeing her struggle gave me confidence to follow. I was not brilliant. I did not think I ever would be good at that sort of thing, but I did better than expected and one of my managers said I put it across very well. It did not provoke a lot of response, which was a bit disappointing, but I felt better when the first session was over and was much calmer on the later sessions. As I paused and changed slides, I would say to myself do well for James, he will be proud of you and, James, please be doing well yourself. He always seemed part of everything I did, it was why I was doing it, he was part of my motivation. He had always been ambitious for himself and us to progress in life as we had not come from privileged backgrounds, in fact the opposite.

We did not go straight back to the hotel that evening; one of the staff very kindly took us for a drive around the city and showed us the sights, including the castle and memorial. It turned out to be late shopping night, so Tony and I decided to have a look in the shops for some Christmas presents. I thought how weary James would sometimes get when we went shopping recently and asked Tony if he was sure he wanted to look in the shops. But he did and we both purchased a couple of presents. I was proud of the little kilt I bought my niece. I do not know why but it gave me a lot of pleasure to buy it. I wished James was with me to share it. It had been so pleasant to relax with someone and not worry about the atmosphere between us. It made me realise how badly something was wrong between me and James. The pleasure had gone out of the simple things that we always did together.

Back at the hotel I rang James before dinner but there was no reply.

Tony and I had another pleasant meal and I put the wine

on my bill that night. The bulk of my efforts were over, although I still had some more to do next day, so I was more relaxed that evening. Tony had the majority to do next day, so when I suggested a drink after dinner, which had gone on longer than we anticipated as we chatted, he declined. I went to the bar alone as I needed a Perrier. It was a busy evening. I had intended sitting there for a couple of minutes to have my drink but when the barman said, "Take it to your room if you like," I did. I rang James again. It was quite late, and I got no reply. I was really feeling uneasy but told myself he was celebrating doing his presentation well. I hoped so much that it had gone marvellously for him. I woke early next morning and was over eager to ring him but made myself wait until I knew the alarm would have gone off. Then I tried; no reply. He must be in the shower, I said to myself. I tried again every fifteen minutes; no reply.

After breakfast I rang his office, they said he was not in yet. I tried once more before I left for the office, just desperately needing to know he was okay and how his day had gone, but he was not in.

I did not get another opportunity to ring him until we were in the departure lounge at Edinburgh but it was not easy to talk from there but I told him I had tried him that morning but he was not there. He said he had left early to take his car to the garage as when he had collected it from them earlier that week, the windscreen wipers did not work. He said they had opened at seven-thirty a.m., and he had got them fixed and gone to work after. I told him I had rung his office and they said he was not in. I did not tell him how many times I had rung. He said his presentation was not too good. It had gone on longer than it was meant to, and he had been incredibly nervous. I felt mean saying mine had gone okay. We were both having to do them again the next week but at different venues, so agreed to improve them together over the weekend. I knew he was not telling me the truth about this morning and his car, but I left the subject as I was looking forward to seeing him again. He agreed to pick me up at Victoria again. When I arrived, the car was there but he was nowhere to be seen. It was absolutely pouring with rain, so I stood there looking around, getting wet and irritated. When he arrived, that warm feeling at seeing him came over me again as usual. Then I looked into his eyes. That look was there again. It was as if he did not like me or want to be with me.

When we got home, I started to unpack and went to the bathroom to replace my washing gear. I thought James had left everything nice; he is usually a bit untidy. Then I looked at the shower, it was dry and clean with the door panel pulled in. It is only ever like that when the cleaning lady has been. That would have been the day before. "Didn't you have a shower this morning?" I asked.

"Of course, I did," he said.

I could not stop saying it; I had to know the truth. "You did not come home last night, did you?" I asked him several times. The Thursday weekly paper had also been behind the door. He kept saying he had been home and had a shower that morning. I knew one hundred percent he was not telling me the truth. He accused me of trying to make something out of nothing, and we got no further. The pain came back in my side; I had to know what was happening between us.

It was my birthday next day; he knew how much I wanted a necklace to replace my favourite one he had bought me, which was stolen in a burglary of our house a few months earlier. I felt sure he would have chosen one similar. I loved the Chanel perfume he did buy for me and tried to cover up my disappointment. He said he wanted to buy me something else that day. I was not in the right frame of mind for shopping. I needed some answers, so I asked him to tell me about Thursday night and what he was hiding. He refused to say anything.

He said he would take me out for a meal that evening, but he had not booked anywhere. We did some more Christmas shopping together that day and when we got back to the car, he did not have his car keys. The spare set was at home; he blamed me, thinking I should have had them in my bag. We had a verbal post-mortem as to where he could have dropped them and retraced our steps around the shops, to no avail. We were about to get the Tube home when I searched the shopping bags and found them in amongst the shopping. I tried to laugh about it but could not get him to respond. He was very morose; so much for a happy birthday, I thought.

We dropped the shopping off at home and got changed. I made a special effort to look good. I was hoping as it was my birthday, we would make love; I really and desperately needed him to want me. He decided to take me to the Ritz for a drink before going for a meal somewhere. Maybe I suggested it, when he just said we could go where I liked. I could not remember later.

Chapter 4
Truth

We were again both under a lot of pressure at work the following week with the presentations to do again. This time mine was in London, an unfriendly office opposed to the objectives of the course. I was very apprehensive. Mine were to take place Monday and Tuesday. James was doing his again on the Friday. I got through mine, I do not know how after the events of the weekend and the feelings inside me. It certainly was not a success, but I did it and felt proud of myself. Others in a similar situation may have called it off but I had always been very responsible over my job.

I wanted to ignore it, but I needed to know about last Thursday and kept asking him about it, but he refused to say anything. Friday morning, I said, "This is the last time I am going to ask. Please tell me or I will find out for myself." I left for work none the wiser, even more desperate to know, and saying sorry for bringing it up on our way to work and wishing him good luck with his presentation. He had not mentioned mine that week or asked how it went. It felt as if he no longer cared about me or my job.

I picked him up from work that evening and he said his presentation had been awful. He said he could not concentrate and had wanted to walk out in the middle. I felt terrible as if I had caused it. We dithered as to whether to go home or eat out.

I preferred to go home, but he seemed to want to eat out as he said he had decided to tell me what I wanted to know. My heart started racing, I felt dizzy and sick. Deep down I knew I did not want to hear it, but at the same time I knew I had to know the truth and face up to what I thought was happening.

Very civilised, we ordered our meal and some wine. Then he started to tell me about this woman he had been seeing for six or seven months. He said how much he cared about her, even loved her. I could not believe it, but I knew it was true. I think I had guessed for some time but hoped I was wrong. How I sat there I do not know. I must have been in a state of shock. I felt damaged, stabbed, ripped apart, broken. I could not believe he would do this to me. My heart was breaking; my body was full of pain. I remember taking my rings off and putting them in the middle of the table, telling him I was no longer his wife. I said he should give them to her if he loved her so much.

I needed to know more, know everything, but at the same time did not want to know. I think I must have been trying to make myself hate him. My love for him would not seem to go away. I felt as if my heart had been taken out, screwed up and put back in. Most of that evening is a daze but it all carried on over the weekend. I asked him questions and got answers, eventually. Each answer was like a blade of a knife cutting a bit more of me away. I got to know her name, where they met, how they spent time together. How much he enjoyed her company, the sex he said was only part of it, so he said. Where she worked, where she lived, what she looked like. I did not know if what he told me was all true. He said she knew he was married; he had told her if it were not her, it would have been someone else. He made it sound as if I was no longer enough for him and maybe never had been. She was willing to have part of him, so she said. He had these needs, he kept telling me. I assumed ones I could not satisfy.

He kept saying loads of men had mistresses and their wives accepted it and were happy, and that is what I should do; just give him the odd night or weekend off when he wanted it.

I knew even if I wanted to, I could not do that. It would destroy me and us and eventually him. I would rather lose him totally than agree to that. I do not think that was the answer he expected. It was as if he did not know me.

Then, he told me he had spoken to her that day and told her he was leaving home before he even told me. I cannot describe how I felt, the room span, I thought I was having a heart attack. I do not know how I did not collapse. He was that close with her that he told her before me. He kept on about how he would still see me, but I had made up my mind – if he had another woman, he would not have me at all because I could not watch that without being destroyed myself. I would have given my life for him but not that way.

I wanted him to go if he needed other women. He kept saying he was not leaving me for another woman, there would be loads of them; he wanted and needed to live a bachelor life. He thought we had been children when we got married and now he needed to try it.

We talked a lot and went around and around in circles, but finally agreed, for the sake of our families who were due to come for Christmas dinner, he would not move out until Boxing Day. I did not want to let our mothers down, especially mine as it was the first Christmas without my father, who had died that year. I did not want to tell them or anyone what was happening. I knew I could not without breaking down. I am so proud I did not want anyone to see that, covering up my feelings again.

Heading up to Christmas was horrendous, the work parties, everyone happy, trying to cover it all up. A few saw I was not myself, but I got through it all. Mainly because he had agreed not to see her until after Christmas and I believed him. He said he rang her and told her he would not call until after Christmas. I carried on plying him with questions about her. I could not stop it. I even asked about the sex – what she did, what he did. The pain and hurt would not get rid of my feelings for him. I thought if I knew more, I would stop feeling so much for him; maybe I could stop loving him. We really had something rare and special and I still felt sure it was on both sides. Maybe wishful thinking.

It had been such a struggle up to Christmas day. When the family arrived, I was busy cooking and it seemed a relief. I was so afraid I would burst into tears. I came so close, but the loo was at hand.

He could not leave Boxing Day as he had to drive his mother over to his brother's, where she was going for lunch, and drive her home again after. We went for a walk around St. James Park together while she was at his brother's. It was lovely, but the tension was there. We talked about it all again, then he suddenly brought up finances. I had not even thought about money, but he had obviously given it a lot of consideration. I gave him a cheque to pay for my half of the standing orders for the next month as they all went out of his bank account. He said we would talk about it later. We had always gone fifty/fifty on everything and never disagreed about money matters.

Saturday arrived; the early part of the day is still a blank.

I had not had much sleep for a fortnight and hardly any that night. I had to force food down; it was jamming in my throat. He started packing. I could hardly breathe at one point. I felt a total failure. I felt I was being thrown away. He offered to stay on his terms, having a girlfriend. I had made up my mind – no matter what, I would not ask him not to go. I was not going to answer any phone calls either. I was not going to see him at all. He had to want me if there was any chance of it being right between us again. My heart knew it could be, or was I kidding myself? I did not seem to know anything for sure. He packed the car and started the engine. My insides were tearing apart, pains shot through my body, the tears came. He turned the engine off, we talked a bit, he said we knew it was coming, we both knew it would be hard. Then he went to go again. I fell against the door, inadvertently. He came back. I crawled to the door, near to collapse, and whispered to him to stay, knowing he could not hear me. He asked me what I said. I did not tell him. We sat together for a bit not saying anything, then he just left.

I was not in control of myself for hours. I sobbed until there was nothing left inside me. The hours passed. I do not think I did anything. I was semi-paralysed; I could not believe we had parted. We had too much to let it go. I eventually dialled his brother's number, totally against my will. He said he was going to stay with him for a while, not with her at the outset. I wanted to beg him to come back, agree to anything, but I knew I could not. I hung up when he answered. I dialled the number again later, desperate, but hung up before it rang. I eventually got to bed; I do not think I slept. I lay there as it got light, desperate for him, unable to get up. "James, James, why oh why," I called, "What did I do wrong; please, please want me again."

I eventually got up and just sat there. I tried to do things but just broke down. The pain was indescribable. I just felt I wanted to die without him. I can now understand how people take their own life over love. The hurt is so bad you just want it to end. I wanted to burn my hand on the hob because I thought that if I felt some external pain, the internal pains might disappear. For the first time, I understood why people self-harm. You need to feel it to know why.

I nearly rang him but forced myself away from the phone. Then the phone rang about four o'clock; I had let the machine answer. It was James; I wanted not to speak to him, but I could not resist it and picked the phone up. He asked to come and see me.

He arrived in less than half an hour. He walked in and burst into tears as I did. I was surprised I had any left. I must have been dehydrated, I had shed too many. We hugged for the first time in a long while. I knew then he still cared enough for me for us to make it again one day. There was no question of him staying, although he said the way he felt all day, he could come back. But we both knew that would not solve anything. He asked for some time. He said, "Maybe we will get back together in time, or we will face up to us not being together but remaining friends." Nothing had really changed apart from me feeling how he felt towards me again. He had not shown it for so long, I did not know why. I had a bit of hope that he knew he still loved me.

He said he had opened his brother's wardrobe to hang up his clothes and there was a picture of me on the door, looking lovely and happy. It had upset him, he said. I could not bear the thought of him being unhappy enough to cry, and my heart went out to him despite what he had done to me. I did not tell him how I felt when I opened the empty wardrobe where his clothes should be. I could not bear it.

He said he wanted me to be strong and go to work next day, give us some time, and see how we felt. I loved him so much and the hate I felt towards the woman who knew he was married and still gave herself to him the second time they met, that is what he told me. I told him again I could not, and would not, share him with another woman. I think he finally accepted it. It felt so good in his arms. I could not believe this was the end of what we had together.

When he left again, I felt a little better, but the sobs just racked through me and the sleep did not come.

I got up next morning; the only thing that got me to work was because he had asked me to go, and I kept telling myself it was for him. I did not do any work, just sat with papers in front of me. I was not myself and people noticed, but I made my usual efforts to hide my feelings and the truth. I wept a couple of times in the toilet and kept telling myself to be strong. He rang me after lunch and told me he had made some decisions and wanted to see me that evening. I asked if he was sure. I too easily agreed for him to come.

He told me he had met her that lunchtime and told her he was not going to see her again. I said to him if he wanted to be alone as he kept saying he did, why did he have to have another woman? He kept telling me it was not about her, it was about him. I think he wanted to show me that it was true. I was glad and felt something change, but I was also afraid he would regret it and resent me for having given her up. I told him that and he said he wanted us to see how we felt, and it was not fair with her in the background. I was not sure he was speaking the truth. I wanted to believe him and did at that moment, but with big doubts in my mind. He could just ring her if he changed his mind, and I knew she would just come running. She sounded that type; he had not seen that, but I had, not even having met her, just from what he had said about her. I knew other women like that willing to be used in the hope of something more. Could I believe him, he had lied to me previously?

He did not have his car, so I drove him over to his brother's house that night. My heart shrivelled when I left him there, and I had to stop around the corner to calm down before I could drive home. I could not breathe properly that night whenever I lay down, so I had no sleep again. I felt awful next morning but managed to get to work. I had to stop myself ringing him all day. Some people made comments about how low or stressed I looked, I felt it too; the tears were hard to keep away. I could not stop myself: late afternoon I rang his office, they said he was not in.

I got home and burst into tears again, despite a tremendous effort not to. I wanted to contact him, but I did not.

I decided I would find out all I could about her. I needed to know. There were ways, and I would find the right person and pay whatever I had to for my own piece of mind.

Chapter 5
New Year

I never really could stand being alone, especially after being with James. I do not think I will be able to stay here in our house. It is so painful. Emotions keep welling up inside of me, no matter how hard I try to suppress them. I have tried so hard; I have been working for three hours, washing, cleaning, ironing. It does not help. I do not think anything will. Maybe with time and practice I can cover it up. I have done it before.

James came last night, New Year's Eve. I had been determined not to get upset. I wanted him to enjoy being with me for the last time. I had had a terrible day at work, trying to cope and cover up my feelings from everyone around me. I know I did not succeed totally. I cooked a special meal for us and enjoyed doing it, as I always had done for James. The table looked lovely and he noticed and said so; there was champagne, which he shared with me, and smoked salmon, followed by steak, asparagus, carrots, and Dijon potatoes. Then, chocolate mousse I had made the night before. One of his favourite menus.

We chatted a bit about us and then other things, but kept returning to us. Well, mainly James and his feelings about us. He said it would not be right for him to come back. That was all I wanted but I did not tell him; there was no way I could accept what he wanted of me. I really believed we could make things right but only if he really wanted to, and I knew he did not. He got irritated at me and I realised later that it was probably because he was tired, but so was I. At the time, I thought he was resenting being here with me and that he wanted to be with her, but it was his suggestion that he came. He wanted us to go out to Trafalgar Square to see the New Year in. He had a lie down while I cleared up and he fell asleep. I went up to him a couple of times just longing to hold him and wanting him to hold me, but I did not touch. I sat downstairs alone for a bit, happy that he was in the house with me but desperately unhappy as well. I wanted him to wake up for midnight, so I went up again. I did not want to wake him, so I just stayed a bit. He woke up and still wanted to go out, so we did. We stopped at Parliament Square and walked over to see throngs of people. Everyone looked happy, with glasses and champagne at the ready. Some had beer but the intention was the same. I seemed to be in a daze. We stood and watched Big Ben strike twelve. You could hardly hear it for the noise. I felt so moved. We kissed; it was a warm meant kiss. We wished each other Happy New Year. It was the first time in my life I could remember not doing 'Auld Lang Syne'; I slowly did it in my head on my own as I held his hand and we walked back to the car. I tried so hard, but something took over my breathing and I could hardly get a breath in my body. I tried consciously to relax and breathe out and weird noises came out of me, a kind of hysteria. I thought I would collapse but I did not want him to see. We got to the car and I sat inside and managed to calm down. We drove home. I cannot remember the route we took. I do remember passing my mother's home, but I could not have gone in. I wished so much my father were still there. To lose both the men I loved in one year was hard to bear. James did the first footing, he said he did not want any champagne. I did not really but I wanted to have a New Year Drink. We both had a small Benedictine. I think he wanted to stay the night, I certainly wanted him to but, again, I did not ask. I had made up my mind not to ask him for anything. Because he had another drink, he said he thought he should stay, so he did. We went to sleep in each other's arms.

I did not want to get up next morning as I knew it bought his leaving for good nearer. We telephoned our mothers and my grandmother from bed and wished them a happy New Year. He kept mentioning breakfast and so I finally got up when he went to the toilet. I asked if he wanted scrambled eggs and bacon, his favourite. He got quite irritated and said he just wanted fruit and coffee. I said as he kept mentioning it, I had thought he wanted a proper breakfast. He said okay, but in that horrible way that made me feel I was making him eat something he did not want. Finally, we did have a nice breakfast and chatted together again.

He emphasised he wanted to see what life was like on his own. I just felt he wanted to get away from me. What had I done, I asked myself, after all this time? I brought her up again; I guessed he was going to live with her. He said repeatedly that he wanted to be on his own. I said I guessed his plan was to wait a bit, then let me know he no longer wanted me, say he had given it a try without someone in the background, then go back to her.

I broke down again and said to him, "You are never going to want to come back, are you?" I hated myself for saying so, but it just happened. He said he did not know.

"Give it time," he kept saying. Was he just giving it time for me to adjust, or did he really want us to consider the possibility of us coming back together again? He did not consider whether I would want him back again. He kept saying he did not want me out of his life, and we would always be friends. I knew that I could never hate him, but I also knew that if there was another woman in his life, I could not share that life with him, even as a friend. At the same time, I could not bear the thought of never seeing him again either and knowing that he was okay. I was being ripped up again. It was as if a fist was inside of me punching the injuries I already had.

It was time for him to go; he said he had his washing and ironing to do. I longed to do it for him but did not say. He said he would call me that evening and see if I wanted to go out for a drink with him. That gave me strength to get through the day just knowing he still wanted to see me. I did my washing and ironing and it tore me apart when there were no shirts, socks, and underpants to put away. Then I got ready for him; I was determined to stay looking nice.

We went out for a meal that evening in Chelsea. It was nice; lovely food and wine. We talked a lot and I felt a bit better being with him. The crunch came again when he left that night. I cannot explain the feeling of ripping apart inside my body and head; I knew I could not sleep so I watched a late-night film and tried again to sleep. I did eventually but woke up with an horrendous nightmare. Spiders were running all over the bed. I did not get back to sleep. I dragged myself to work next day; I tried to start with a determined effort when I got there but it did not take long before the tears tried to well up. Most of my efforts that day went into suppressing them. I could not tell anybody. I gave up on the way home as tears streamed down my face.

At home I thought to myself, you must make an effort. I

had just started doing something when the doorbell rang. It was James' brother. He had come to pick up the chairs we had borrowed for Christmas Day. He asked if I had a cold and I said yes, but really it was the remains of the crying. He loaded the chairs in his car and came back. I offered him a drink, hoping he would say no, which he did. Then he asked if I was okay and how long he thought this thing with James would last. I did not know how much he knew. I just burst into tears and said I did not know. He comforted me and told me he knew how I felt. His partner of fifteen years had left him for someone else a few years before. He told me when it happened, he had smashed up his kitchen and since then none of the pan lids fitted the pans. I asked if he felt better afterwards and laughed.

We chatted a while, but I did not tell him very much. I did not want anyone to know how hurt and upset I was. He said I ought to make James say what he was doing, as it was not fair to me to sit waiting for him to decide and coming over when he wanted to. I said I did like seeing him and was just giving him some time to sort himself out. I kept telling him not to let me hold him up; I did not really want to talk to him in case I told him too much, although I knew he was trying to help me. He was genuinely nice and told me to ring him at work if I needed anything. He left and I decided to take all the decorations down; I did not want the tree there any more or the cards. I never wanted to be reminded of this Christmas again. I threw lots of things away. I could not eat, and I felt sick. I forced a few nuts down and felt even worse. I had just finished clearing everything away when the phone rang. It was James. I did not want to but I broke down over the phone. He started talking about his needs again and how he went home early and was pissed off. I felt he was regretting not seeing her and asked if he was going to start again. He said, "Why not, she is available." I hung up because I could not speak and the room was spinning; how hurtful could he be? He rang back and said he was coming round. I told him I did not want to see him here, but he came anyway.

He then told me he had a choice of coming back now, which he did not want to do; he was staying away because he wanted to do what he chose. I asked if he was saying he meant to go back to her, and it was lies that it was just about his needs. He was trying to see me at the same time. He avoided answering and would not admit to it, but odd things he said made me feel he was sorry he had rushed into not seeing her. I do not think now that he really cared about her but liked her for the company and the sex. At the time, I was not sure what he felt for her or me. I did not think it would last with her, but I knew I would not be seeing him while he saw her. It would be better to split now.

He finally told me he was not going to come back any time soon and I had to accept that. He said he wanted to get a flat and try it on his own. I knew that already.

We talked and things got a little better. He told me there were things he wanted to tell me about himself and that he would one day. He admitted he had stopped me being myself, and had lived with regrets and guilt since the last time he had another woman. He had done this before, and he had given her up because I found out. Why did he not accept and say that before, I wondered?

I kept wondering what he was going to tell me and wondering if, somehow, I had driven him away from me. If I had, I needed to know. Maybe I could ask him and get a true and full answer one day. I do love him so much and had always done what I did because of that love. He left again and said he would see me next day. I asked if he was sure that was a good idea. He seemed to really want to and so I agreed. I just hoped it was not because he felt sorry for me; that was the last thing I wanted.

James seemed to think the hurt would go away in time. How wrong can one be? I knew it never would, but maybe I could learn to cover it up a bit better. I had done it before. I was not sure how much inner strength I had left, it felt destroyed, maybe it could grow again.

He asked me to tell him what I wanted but I could not. I was not totally sure. I knew I wanted us to build together as I always had; I wanted us to contribute together to us, to the world, to anyone close. I wanted us to grow old together, happy and contented in what we had done and achieved together. Perhaps I wanted too much togetherness. I wanted us to act separately as well, but with each other's strength and support behind us. We had it once. I cannot believe after all that we have been through and knowing we still love and care for each other, that we cannot get it back. Please God, if there is one, help us to find each other again. The world needs more people to have that to survive and succeed in the future.

Why does there seem to be so much time today? With him there, it seemed to be so little time on a Saturday. What on earth can I do? I have hoovered. I have bathed. I have shopped. I met my brother by chance. The first thing he said is, "Where is James?"

I just said, "Working today," and held back the tears. Maybe I should have told him, but I could not. I feel such a failure. I suppose I am ashamed. I do not really know why. I have not done anything to be ashamed of, but that is how I feel.

Did I depend on him too much? I did not mean to; maybe I took too much out of him. I need to believe there is a chance for us together again or I will just give up. Am I still living off his strength even though he is not here? Perhaps I am not being fair to him. I will try and put on a strong front when he comes tonight. He will be here in about four hours. I can spend some time preparing him a meal. I still seem to trust him but there is a doubt in the background. Is he pretending he is not seeing her and when he says he hopes we will come together again happily, or is he just trying to be kind to me? If he is not being truthful and I will have to face it later, I know I will not be able to pretend to anyone any longer. Not even myself. I really believe we were different, that was my strength, if I am proved wrong, I can feel my strength draining away. Please do not let me be wrong about us. I know it is there, that special something that nothing can destroy, not even death. Please let it defeat the rest and bring us happiness again. Please. I will have to try to be strong for him; if we cannot be happy together, it is better he is happy without me than we are both unhappy. I truly do not believe he will ever be contented without me, but perhaps that is a selfish feeling. I only ever wanted to make him happy. I did for a long time but sometime, somewhere, it went wrong. I should have tried harder to find out what he needed from me. When you have become part of someone else instead of yourself, it is hard to understand when the need for that part changes. I think maybe that is what happened. He certainly does not want me currently as his wife, and I must adapt to that. It will probably be the hardest thing I ever did in my life. If that is what he wants and needs of me. I will try. Maybe it would be easier if I did not have the love and affection and respect that I do for him. I have not told him about the respect for a long time. It did not go away, but I needed a sign from him that he was not full of regrets over what happened before with the previous woman I found out about. I think that affected me more than I have acknowledged. I pretended I had forgiven him but maybe I did not. Perhaps that has caused this to happen now. I have been too proud to tell him how I felt and how it hurt. I tried to show him, but I think I failed and drove him away again.

I need to find some strength from somewhere to get through the next few months. I do not know where to start. I am trying to carry on with my life and job, but something is weighing down on my throat and stomach and sapping all my effort. My legs feel like jelly. I cannot concentrate on what I am doing. I will keep trying – for us.

James came again tonight. It was a week since he left. It was only Tuesday he had not come for a visit. I had not asked him to come once, he seemed to want to. I was glad; I would not have let him if I knew he was still seeing her, but I wanted to see him so much and to feel him touch me. It was so important.

I gave him a nice meal again and we shared some wine. We chatted again and he told me about his pain over it all. He said it was like having a tooth pulled out without anaesthetic. I wondered, if that was the case why he was doing it all? I knew he loved and cared for me still. He said he knew he did but he had to be sure he wanted to come back, and we should look on it as a temporary separation. I suppose, because I wanted to believe him at that point, I did and promised to be strong for us. I even said maybe some good would come out of it all and give us something we did not have before. Maybe it would.

Then he said the meal was excellent and I did not need to use all the best cutlery and china for him. I said I had wanted to. He said, "You enjoy cooking for me, don't you?"

"I always have," I replied, "But you did not get this treatment when you lived here very often," and smiled.

He said, "You are just the kind of girlfriend I am looking for. Attractive, nice personality, lovely home, a responsible job, own car." Then he said, "I would much rather see you once or twice a week and be happy than see you every day and be unhappy." I did not disagree but wondered if he knew how much that hurt me.

We decided it was a good idea to go to the cinema. I picked the film 'Heartbreak Ridge' with Clint Eastwood. I did not know exactly what it was about, but it turned out the main theme was American Cadets, but in the background was Clint Eastwood looking for his ex-wife to get back with him when he left the army. They did.

We came home after and he had a drink. I did not want him to leave and I do not think he wanted to go. We fell asleep on the sofa and woke about one-thirty a.m. I asked if he wanted to stay but he eventually decided to leave, and I went to bed alone.

I did not sleep well again and just did not want to get up in the morning. I felt I had nothing to get up for. I just lay in bed but did not sleep.

The phone disturbed me at about twelve-thirty p.m. It was my neighbour. "Is everything all right?" she asked. "Things are different," she said. I do not know what she had seen.

"Fine," I said, "No problem."

She said, "The car comes and goes at odd times and we were worried one of you was ill, or one of your parents, and you had not told us."

"Oh, no," I replied. I just said, "James has a big job on at present, everything is fine."

"You would tell us if anything is wrong?" she said.

"Oh yes," I replied.

"Are you lonely when he is not home?" she asked.

"No, I am busy working," I lied. I hated lying to people, I always did.

"Well, if you are, please come and see us," she said, "We are always here for you." I thanked her and assured her that all was okay. We wished each other Happy New Year. She asked me to tell James she had rung. I said I would. That really disturbed and upset me, so I got up and forced some breakfast down. I was not even enjoying that any more. I felt he would not contact me today so knew I just had to get on. I thought of trying to get a game of squash, my main hobby, but it was just not in me.

I read the paper but did not seem to take much in. There was an article on Harold Macmillan which, for some reason, made me sad. A lot of the content reminded me of the old James. I am not sure now what or why, but it did. A man to be great and different. Incredibly special, that was how he was to me. I watered my plants. I sat and kept imagining, or perhaps longing, for the day when James would knock on the door and ask to come back. Please let it be, I said to myself as I suppressed the churning emotions inside me.

I tried to talk myself into making efforts at work so nobody would know. I thought of what I could do in the evenings and at weekends. Perhaps some French lessons, play squash, work in the house. Just be strong, I thought, so you are ready when he wants to come back. I kept avoiding the 'if'. I read the Sunday magazine and found the perfect rack for all his ties, and thought of sending off for it. I did not but saved the magazine to show him. Maybe I would send for it later.

The phone rang and I could not answer it. I let the machine pick up, but nobody spoke. It unnerved me and set me shaking again. I wish I could stop it. There was no reason for it. Perhaps I could finish the bottle of wine we started last night to calm me down.

I turned the TV on; it only lasted ten minutes. The picture shrank to six inches. I turned it off and on again; it lasted two minutes and disappeared. The day before, the blinds in the bathroom had broken, the day before that a tassel on the bedroom blinds had fallen off. Was our home going to collapse around me? It seemed to need him as well. I got terribly upset again after trying so hard not to all day.

Despite my strong intentions I knew I was not holding up too well. I had to just keep going and doing my best. I seemed to have been struggling to do that for so long. I desperately needed to call him but knew I must not. I tried to eat a little food, but it made me feel sick. How things can change.

I said to myself, if you do not cope he will never come back to you. I had to believe that to convince myself of it to give me the strength I needed to carry on. How many more days would I have to endure this tearing pain that I could not even begin to describe? You would have to feel it to know. I wonder if it is the heart breaking. If so, could it ever be repaired?

Effectively we had separated. I could not bring myself to tell a single soul. I was brought up to be independent, look after myself and sort your own problems out. I just kept it to myself and tried my best to carry on.

Chapter 6
Keeping Going

I do not know how I got through today. I think the phone call saved me. I went to work and made a concerted effort to get into it; I had so much to do. The worst thing, to prepare another presentation for next week. If I had to do it today, I would have failed. I know my mind was wandering from what I was doing. My body seemed to drag me away from my work. It was pulling me. I wanted to talk to him, to know he was okay, how he had been yesterday. I knew I had to stop myself calling; he did not want me now, therefore I had to wait for him to call me, I kept telling myself that. I did not seem able to control myself; I nearly rang and said I would agree to anything if he came back, even fifty girlfriends; I ached so much, my insides seemed to be exploding with needs and love and other things I didn't understand myself. There were moments if anyone had come into my office, I could not have held back the emotion in me. Luckily for me, nobody came at the worst moments, but everyone knew there was something wrong with me and I wanted to cover it all up. I did not want to talk to anybody. I did not want any advice. I know what I wanted – no matter what happened I loved him so much. I went out at lunchtime to stop myself calling him. When I came back, the feelings were still in me and I just did not seem to be in control of myself. I forced myself to do some work on the computer because it was in an office with other people, which seemed to help me cover it all up. He rang while I was in another room, so I went back to mine and spoke to him; just talking to him made me feel better, and he said he wanted to come again that evening. I could not refuse. I offered to cook a meal again for him and he accepted. How is it possible to feel so much for somebody else, care so much for them, even more than you do for yourself? That is how I currently felt; could that have caused our problems? I just did not know. I felt better knowing he was coming; how would I feel when he left again? Should I be trying not to care for him so much? I just did not know.

I felt so different when he came, so much better; I was just devastated when he left but I think I had more hope. He had spoken about how he could come back. It was how he felt now, but in two weeks' time he may feel differently. "Give us time," he said. "We are not enemies, we are still friends; we are not going out of each other's lives. Ring me if you want anything." I wanted him but I knew I could not ring him for that.

He told me I might feel differently if I thought about how it was before he left. How he had been towards me when we went to visit my brother for the weekend, and other times. He often behaved in an unreasonable and thoughtless way if we were doing something I had chosen, as if he wanted to spoil it. If I was honest, things had not been right since his previous affair. It was as if he had been making me pay for giving her up.

He said I needed to talk to someone about everything that is happening, but I did not want to. I wanted to sort my own feelings out, not get others views and do it for me. I am different and independent. I want to live by my answers of myself not someone else's views on my problems as if they were their own. We are all individuals who feel differently. Common feelings maybe, but nobody could feel about James as I do just as no one else has my fingerprints. More people should understand that and maybe better solutions to their own problems would be found.

I slept a little better that night although I knew it was not enough; I was exhausted, it seemed to be catching up with me. I started next day a lot better, feeling more confident that he might want to come back, give her up and see us happily together again. As the day progressed, I got lower again as doubts crept in. Was he just trying to get me used to the idea gently that he was never coming back, never wanted me as his wife again? Did he want me to build a life for myself to be ready for when he told me? I think if that is true, it would be better if he told me now. If I survive with the hope that we will be as we should be again, then find out that we will not, it would be more devastating and harder to cope with than it is now. Please do not let that be. He seemed to feel when I was at my lowest point – the phone rang. He asked me if I wanted to meet him for a McDonald's after his game of squash. I readily agreed. Perhaps it would help more if I were not so eager. I do not know; I do not feel sure about anything. I think I was beginning to think it would be better with no contact at all from him.

I went to a meeting at work today; I would normally contribute a great deal. Crisis management time, looking for solutions, was what I excelled at. The answers were in my head, but I did not give much; the little I did was used. My mind kept wandering away from the topic. I ended up trying to concentrate on the people attending, spotting those who had been hurt and how it showed in the way they reacted to things.

I did not want to become like that. I guessed there were two of them – it showed in their eyes. Perhaps it was also now in mine.

We talked yet again that evening; he said it would be no good if he came back just because I was desperate for him. I asked him if he was seeing me because he wanted to or because he felt sorry for me. He said it was the same thing, but I knew it was not. He explained again he just did not want to be married at the current moment in time; he wanted another way of life. He said either way, he was giving up something he wanted. Just give it time, he kept saying. How long, I wondered, could I give it? I did not feel it would get any easier, although we seemed to talk more calmly about it, and I seemed less upset. That was true on the surface only.

Underneath all the pain and emotion, my feelings for him were still there and occasionally, they would all churn around inside of me until I could not bear it any longer. Even I did not know how much I felt for him until now. If anyone had told me all this could happen and I would still love and care about him as I did, I would not have believed it. I felt it now.

I may regret what I have done tonight for the rest of my life, but I feel it was right or things would have just deteriorated between us. The odds were against it coming right. Yesterday evening was horrendous; he came again, just to pop in, he said. We chatted as we had been doing, I felt he was not telling me something, then I asked what he was doing next day. I think I wondered if he was going to see her. We were both tired and he got irritable. He started saying how bad things had been over the past few years, making it sound as if we had been bitter enemies, at each other's throats; it had never really been like that. We had not been as close as before he had the previous affair, but it was not as he described it. He made me feel as if he had been coming round because he felt sorry for me and was worried about me. He accused me of trying to blackmail him into staying with me. It was not true because I knew I did not want that. I knew I wanted him back more than anything in the world but only if he wanted me. I ended up sobbing and hardly able to breathe, then apologising for getting upset. I felt so hopeless and saw that I was just a burden to him. He needed me off his back. I did not sleep again that night and was beginning to look awful. I am not sure when I decided, I think it was when he rang to say he was coming again, that I had to give something more to him and I must not get upset when he visited, no matter what. I do not think I pre-decided my action, but I felt in a turmoil again as soon as he arrived. I told him we could not carry on as things were; he agreed, he said I was hanging onto him as if he still lived with me. He said when he was with me, he wanted to come back home, but he knew in a couple of weeks he would regret it and needed time. I do not know how I told him without emotion in me exploding, but I said he should just go and do what he wanted. I told him not to contact me or worry about me each day but to go and try whatever it was he wanted and needed. He said he would still call and/or see me. I said it depended on his way of life whether I wanted to see him or not. We got back to the subject of her and I said I thought he had made up his mind to contact her again. That was if he had not already been doing it. He said again it was nothing to do with her, he just wanted another way of life. I quite calmly pointed out that it was about her. I had asked him to leave because he wanted her in his life, and I was not prepared to share my life with a man who had another woman, however much I loved him. He went on about her being willing to accept him part time. He said he had been watching other blokes who only saw their girlfriends once or twice a week, and that was what he wanted – not to live with anyone.

I felt whatever I said would not stop him contacting her again but something, that inner feeling, told me to tell him to think about it. I think I knew he was still in contact with her anyway, despite what he said to me. I had received several phone calls where the person hung up when I answered. I am sure it was her, but I did not think he would believe me if I told him, so I did not. There were a couple when she spoke pretending to be someone else with a wrong number, but I knew.

He was to have an interview for a promotion shortly and I did not want the fact he was seeing her to jeopardise the outcome, so I told him to be careful what he did. I admit that was only part of it. The thought of him being with her doing our things, sharing with her, was opening my stomach as if I were being operated on whilst awake. But I could only suggest to him that he thought hard about what he was doing before he acted. It was totally my feeling and jealousies, but it was something I needed to warn him about, but I think I was wasting my time. If he did not do it now it was just putting off the day. He wanted to set a date to contact me, but I did not want any commitments. He said he did not want me hanging up on him or turning horrible, and that he would still be seeing me. I said I did not want to see him if he was going to be like the previous evening towards me, which had left me uncontrollably upset. If the life he was going to lead would make me feel like that, it was better for both of us that we did not meet at all. Especially if I could not ask what he had been doing. I did not want any more lies; he agreed. I did not want any half-truths either, or words under the carpet; he said he agreed. That was it, I was on my own and he would be seeing her again. I think he had been seeing her anyway and just lying to me.

We did not make any commitments to meet, but our twentieth wedding anniversary was coming up in three months and he said we would meet before that. I did not think it was going to be something to celebrate and I did not think I would survive without seeing him, but I would not admit to that. I said I knew people I would not mix with because I did not like their way of life and if what he did made me feel like that, I would be better never seeing him again. I knew I would never be better not seeing him, but equally I could not cope with him telling me about his times with her, but then I also felt I needed to know. I was not going to come out of this too well whichever way it went. Unless he decided he did not need another woman, I knew we were finished. I could only hope, but knew he could not just decide; that he would have to find out for himself, I hoped.

I do not know how my body stood the strain of trying to be strong that evening. I even admitted to him that the easiest thing would be for me to shut myself in the house every evening and weekend, but I was not going to. I told him I was going to get a social life going again as I would be a single woman. I would get out and about a bit so if he called, I might not be in. I wanted to be able to do those things and would try, although all I wanted to do was sleep and not wake up to ease the pressure inside my head. I told him these things so I would not need to answer the phone. I could let the machine take the calls. Then I could put off his telling me what he had been doing. The things I needed and had to know. I do not know why, but I did not want to hear. He finally left after I agreed to look after him the night before his interview for his promotion. It was so important to him and me; I felt he would get the job but there was a danger of it being jeopardised. I really hoped he would be successful. I always had done; we had worked hard as a couple to get where we are. He always seemed so much better and above everyone around us, maybe only in my eyes, but I do not think so. I always knew he was incredibly special, had something special. Even before it grew, and he realised himself. Even now, he did not know what it was and was maybe on the path to losing a big part of it. I hoped I was doing the right things to help him get it back and us back. I was special as well, especially to him once. As a team we could not fail.

I thought I was having a heart attack when he left. I think it was just the strain of covering up how I really felt, and telling him to do the things I could not bear to think of him doing. The pains shot across my chest and down my side. The room wobbled and I felt sick. I lay down. I was terribly afraid I would pass out, I think that is what kept me conscious; I was too ill to even cry, or was afraid to exert myself any more, I am not sure. No tears came – perhaps I should have let them. It was a long time before I could get up; when I looked in the mirror, I was grey. The pains went through to my back, but they were still now instead of moving. Could I let him do this to me, I thought? I might have died, or was I exaggerating? I still felt if I did anything or moved quickly, I would pass out. I went to bed unable to analyse how I felt, what I felt, what I should or could do. I felt desperately alone, more lonely than

I had ever been in my whole life, but unable to do anything about it at that point in time. If my time was up, I thought, and they were ready for me, I would have died that night.

Those people who have trained themselves not to feel, if that really is what they have managed to accomplish, maybe they have just managed to put on a good front, have done themselves a service. The pressures that covering the truth I felt that night in my body, were like one imagines in a compression chamber, out of control, or when crushed alive by a heavy weight. You could only ever take it once. I would not have to try again.

I could not believe how I felt today, very shaky but with an inner calm. It was as if a bomb had exploded beside me and I was injured but knew I would survive and be okay.

He arrived again one evening without having let me know; he said he wanted to talk so I let him in. I was slightly hopeful he wanted to be with me again, without her. I still did not believe his excuse – it was not about her, and he just needed a life on his own because we had married too young and he needed some freedom. He had come to tell me he had decided to buy a flat he had found, and move in on his own. He assured me not with her; I just listened. He said he wanted to buy it in joint names with me, so I did not need to worry he was trying to rip me off financially. We had always earned about the same and had shared everything, and had a joint account for our savings. We had been savers not spenders, so we had a reasonable sum together. Then he said I might at some time want to move from our house which was jointly owned, and we would share the value of the two properties. I said extraordinarily little – he had taken me by surprise. He left, asking me to think about it.

All I could think of when he had gone was how I could afford to keep my home; we had worked so hard together to get it. If this was the way it was going, I decided I wanted to buy him out. There was no way I wanted to go backwards to how we lived as children in council flats. I wanted my own house. I did not have long as he said he needed to purchase the flat before it got sold to someone else. I knew he would buy the property whatever I said so I agreed; it would be put in joint names on condition that when it came to it, I could buy him out of our current home. He agreed verbally and I trusted that he would keep his word. I knew it would be tight and difficult for me in the future, but I had a good job and salary and would be able to get a mortgage on my own. If it came to it, I could easily let one of the spare bedrooms to someone at work to help pay for it. I agreed to look at the flat with him, although I had no interest in it at all. It was close to his office so I assumed he would be taking his women to it. His purchase went ahead, and he took some items from our home to furnish it, but also purchased some cheapish furniture to make it habitable. I personally never wanted to go near it or have anything to do with it. I was just thinking about safeguarding my finances.

I then told him he had basically left me. I wanted the keys to our house so he could not come and go as he pleased, and I did not want to see him at all. It just gave me hope when he came and called and then the devastation when he left again. He had an absurd idea we could remain friends and meet regularly. I think I said something like: you want me to change places with your slag, she will be living with you not me. Again, he denied he was leaving for her, and said he needed to be on his own and have a different life. So, we parted.

I carried on like a zombie, working as best I could though

not to my usual standards. Pretending to anyone close, or who asked, that he was away working again. This was not unusual. I ate and slept badly though I tried to stay healthy, but lost a lot of weight I could not afford to. I had got used to him working away sometimes so I had a lone routine. It was not easy, but inside I think I am strong mentally if not physically. I did not tell a soul.

However much it hurt, there was a need in me to know everything. I had learnt how to find out the last time and that is what I did. It was the phone calls that prompted me to do it. He must have told her where I worked because I started getting the odd call there, as well as at home. I would answer and there would be nothing, and then they hung up. I knew it was her; I think she wanted me to know so I would not want him. I did not know what he had told her, but I knew she wanted us apart forever. I found out where she worked, what she did, where she lived, and a bit about her past affairs. She seemed to like married men from what I learned. I wondered if James knew that. When I saw her from a distance, I wanted to tackle her but decided against it. Maybe later I would.

I accepted inside that he had hurt me too much for it ever to be the same again, even if I still believed we had true love and that it would, or should, have lasted forever. I told myself to accept I had lost that love and had to get on with life without it. I knew there were things I needed to do. Let the family and others know and sort out my finances, separate everything from him. I had not yet reached the point where I could do it with a strong front. I had to wait until I had built myself back up a bit. I was working on it. It had been many weeks and I had good and bad days, but I was a strong lady and determined to keep myself strong.

Chapter 7
Decision Time A Few Months Later

I had been getting much stronger, working at it, more my old self. I was getting ready to tell my family and friends. Not telling people was getting more difficult as time went on. I had some good days when I was positive about my future, but I had some bad and sad ones as well. I had resigned myself to him being happier without me and I did not begrudge him that. I knew I was damaged in my heart and head, but I knew I could overcome it and live with the scars, so long as I did not see or hear from him.

Yesterday had been one of the worst bad days, I think, although it is hard to be sure afterwards. I went to work. Luckily, I had booked the afternoon off to have my hair cut. I would not have got through the whole day without letting myself down. Everyone I spoke to seemed to give me an odd look and I was on the verge of tears every time I spoke, despite my determination not to let anyone know about my problems. I was trying extremely hard to be strong and get on with my lonely life. I had some days where I felt I was coping well. I disappeared to the loo for about twenty minutes to try and sort myself out. I kept wondering if having told him to go was the biggest mistake of my life. Perhaps I could not bear the pain I would be going through, and it would destroy all that we had left if I had not done it. Then I would convince myself that I had no alternative; he had convinced me he had to try this other way of life or he would never be happy and never want to come back. I had always had the feeling he knew he would want to come back one day. Now I wondered if I would still want him, knowing that he had chosen to have another woman, or women, whichever it turned out to be. I knew in my heart I would always want him as my husband but would I be able to put it behind me? It depended on what he did, how much he told me and how much he enjoyed it. I just did not know how I would stand up to knowing he was sharing his life, his feelings, his thoughts, maybe his love (although he had tried to convince me he did not love her), with someone else. Just the thought of it, even before it was happening, was affecting me in a way which I had not believed could ever happen to me. I could feel myself crumbling, not only physically but mentally, and I was unable to control it or do anything about it. I began to wonder if people who did not care about others were better off. I knew I was wrong but then sometimes thoughts just come to you. I think for one minute I even thought it would be better if he had died, although I never wanted him to be dead, instead of leaving me as he was. I hated myself even for the thought.

I left work in a daze and went to the hairdresser. She politely asked me if I was okay, and said I looked tired and thin since she had last seen me. I think she really meant how dreadful I looked. I was pale and thin with bags under my puffy eyes. You see everything in the hairdresser mirror. I even had the shakes some of the time. I looked better when I left, having rested for a couple of hours, and my hair looked good. I could not face going home to an empty house. I had promised to visit my mother but knew I could not see her without showing how I felt, and I was not ready to tell her we had split up. I went to the sales to try and brighten myself up. I knew it would not work but I bought some trousers and a suit that I could not really afford, in view of the circumstances. I walked through the men's department and got choked up, wanting to look and buy something for James. I had always done that. Someone knocked into me and apologised, I nearly burst into tears and left.

I drove home the long way round and in traffic jams just to delay getting there. When I arrived home his car was there. I had not seen or spoken to him for quite a while since he had said it was nothing to do with her and he was living a bachelor life. I had told him I did not want to see or hear from him while any other woman was taking my place. Although he had said it was not about her and he would probably not see her very often. I was both glad and disappointed and afraid. As soon as I saw him, I knew he wanted to tell me something. He said he had been concerned as to where I was as he had called the office to ask if he could come, and they told him I had left at lunchtime. He said he had been waiting for me for two hours. I did not tell him where I had been or what I had been doing. I felt like saying it was none of his business, but I did not.

I let him in, and he said he had decided he wanted to come back if I would have him. I should have felt elated, it was all I wanted to hear, but there were all these doubts inside me. I had to ask. What about her, his wants, his needs that he kept talking and telling me about. He told me he had seen her that day and told her they were finished, and he was going to ask me if he could come back. So, he had confirmed he had still been seeing her regularly. I was angry and hurt that he had told her anything about me and us. He said it was because he could not get hold of me and he had promised to tell her what he had decided. Then I knew he had been lying to me again and had still been seeing a lot of her. He had said he was going to try life on his own, another lie. I did not know whether to believe him now. He said he had thought hard about it, written down for and against for his three alternatives: us, her or alone. He told me he could not do it to me, and that he had realised how much he cared about us and what we had together. I still had a big doubt about it all and whether he was telling the truth, but I could not bring myself, at that point, to say no to him coming back. I felt I could not be sure about him not trying to see her behind my back, or her trying to contact him, or him even doing it again with someone else. I could not just say yes either without lots of reassurances. I might have to go through all this again and it would kill me as a person.

I had immersed myself in work, not as positively as normal, but I was coping Monday to Friday. The weekends were the most difficult and lonely. I had still not told a single person so it was difficult for me to see anyone or have visitors without knowing I would crumble and tell them, so I put them off. It was easy to tell people James was away working when he was not around as this was a normal habit with his job. I had to be careful at work in a male environment, where any weakness would lead to my colleagues using the female card to undermine me. I did have females in my team at work, but I was the boss and it would be difficult to confide in them. The contact with him again after all this time was weakening and touching my need for company.

I had grown a bit stronger again, not back to the woman I had been previously, but I was coping, although I did have low days like today. I had started to realise I would survive on my own even if it was not what I wanted. I felt more devastated for him because I felt he did not realise what he was throwing away. I knew he would never find another love like mine; it was meant to be from day one. Better to have loved and lost than never to have loved at all. Despite the wreckage I believed that was right. I had also recognised that my emotional survival was critical to me; I would not let him destroy me; I was a very capable lady and had always been healthily independent in many ways.

I had huge reservations, did not totally believe that he was prepared to finish with her and other women. I also knew I would regret just saying no.

Together we agreed we could not change what had happened or change the past, and we would work together to build up what we have and enjoy life together again. I was full of what ifs, huge doubts, and questions about if he was being honest. I did not say yes but I agreed we would try. Deep down I did not think it would work. I did not think I would ever trust him again or believe he was not lying to me. The scars were too deep. I know scars can heal but they never disappear.

After a while, and lengthy discussions, we went together and picked some of his clothes up from his flat. I thought, has she been here and what did they do when they were together, but I did not say and tried to be positive. I was still in a turmoil. I asked if he was going to change his mind, if he was sure, if he had rushed into a decision, if he needed more time. He said he was sure about what he was doing. I asked for the truth about his contact with her and he eventually told me that she had contacted him to find out where she stood with him, and he had told her he was deciding and would let her know today. She had got upset over him finishing with her and had threatened to do something stupid, and he was now worried about her committing suicide. I know from what he had told me and what I had found out about her, she was not the type to do that, more likely get drunk and take up with the first bloke to come along. He obviously still cared a bit about her. He said he felt sorry for her and guilty about what he had done to her. He kept telling me he told her from the beginning he was married. I learnt a bit more about her, still very painful but accepting I had to hear. She had previously been let down by blokes several times. He also confirmed what I knew that she had been with married men before. He also confirmed he had bought her the same Christmas present as me. I had seen that when the credit card statement came through and I had thrown my present away. A few things came out in our discussions which seemed to go from one aspect to another. Her, him coming back, things that had happened between them. I could not get really focused on what I needed to say and do. I do not think it crossed his mind that I may not want him back.

He wanted to ring her and check she was okay as it had all happened that afternoon. I was not happy but reluctantly agreed. I did not want to stop him, even though I knew it would give her hope and a reason to still cling onto him if she could. He assured me it was totally over and there was no way it would start again whatever happened between us. But always a but – he told her he would be there as a friend if she needed one. I had to tell him I would never be happy or accept that, and it would not work between us if he was still in contact with her behind my back. He agreed it would be out in the open if anything happened. There was no reply when he rang her phone, so he started to think the worst and suggested he went to look for her in the pub where they used to meet. Or at the station. He seemed to think she might be sitting in the station or drinking too much somewhere. I knew again she would not be. I said she is on her way home. I said if he really wanted to go looking, he need not bother to come back. An alternative would be to take me along with him, but I did not want to see her again. I had already watched her when I knew who he was seeing. I did not care a damn about her, but I also did not wish her any harm. I am not like that. I persuaded him to wait a bit and try her again later, which he did, and she was there. I listened and he told her he was just making sure she was okay and had not done anything stupid. I could not hear what she said but I could tell she was trying to have a conversation with him, and James could not reply properly as he wanted to because I was there. He just said he had to go and was glad she was home okay, and had not done anything silly to let herself down. He told me she said she was not okay; it sounded to me as if she was trying to hang onto him with threats of being unable to cope and doing stupid things. He then told me how, when he met her, she was low because someone had just finished with her, she was drinking alone, and he had helped her through it. They both now wished they had not got involved with sex and just stayed as friends. Too late, I thought, they only felt like that because they had been found out and we had all been hurt, me the most. He did not tell me a lot about her that I had not already learnt myself. Some through asking people, some from my subconscious; I wish I could do it to order and know how it worked. She was not really a horrible person – a bit pathetic and desperate to find a partner, even if a married one.

I was surprised it had not taken him longer to decide to try and come back. It had been nearly four months. I thought it would be longer before he realised what he was losing and get fed up with what he was gaining. I was wrong. Perhaps because I pushed it by telling him to go and try it all if he wanted it so badly, and stopped letting him just visit and call me, I do not know. At that moment I was so glad there is a chance to try. Untold damage to us may have been done that is unrepairable. Maybe it already had anyway because of the last time before this happened, whatever caused it all.

We did not suddenly fall into each other's arms and make passionate love. I could not let myself, even if we had wanted to; every day I was reading about AIDS. I knew he did not have it, but I had to know he had been checked for anything else before I could be relaxed about it. He accepted that after the last time he understood how I felt. We both knew all would not come right tomorrow or next week, but we both felt that when or if it did, maybe we would benefit from it in the end and be stronger together than we were before. I wonder and I hope because I thought we were unbreakable together. Things had never really been right since I found out about the previous woman several years before. I now know I should have chucked him out then rather than accept it had just been a fling. We had both, maybe without realising, never quite recovered from it.

At the back of my mind I thought, does he really think I am just going to take him back because he has changed his mind? Maybe it was not as good with her as he thought. This will never work but I suppose I should give it a trial, or I might regret it later.

I wondered if I would regret the lost opportunities I had missed to spend time with other men. I had had lots of temptations. I had been asked out several times, but they all knew I was married and did not know I was separated. I had wanted to say yes on some occasions as I liked the company of men. But I just knew inside I was still married and did not want to sleep with anyone else. I would need to be divorced to do that. I did try but my problem was I was still in love and, despite having accepted he no longer loved me, there was a glimmer of hope in the back of my mind he would come back. This was despite me convincing myself I would not have him back even if he wanted me. Quite a dilemma at the time.

PART TWO
BEFORE

Chapter 8
First Lies

It was several years ago that I had first been hurt, but I had come through it because I believed him. I also believed it would never happen again.

The feelings now were not the same as last time I had been through something like this. Some of the feelings were there but others were new, and some had disappeared. Perhaps it was because this time I knew it could happen to me, to us. It had happened before but last time beforehand, I had been one hundred percent confident it would never come to something like that with us; I had suspected with all his travelling, he might have a casual affair if it was on offer as most men would, but not to jeopardise what we had with a long term regular relationship. I always thought that women who did not kick their man into touch after something like that, were weak and too accepting.

Again, at that time. I had known for a while that all was not right. It was so difficult with him working away from home Monday to Friday and trying to put our whole relationship into the weekend. Perhaps that was one of the causes of the problem. I should have let the weekends just be weekends – perhaps I was at fault there.

I think there was a time we just fell into each other's arms and made love every weekend when he returned. We were an incredibly happy couple, always in love and happy to be together. There started to be some weekends when we did not make love. Sometimes, there just did not seem to be the time when we were not both too tired. It did not stop altogether but I felt it was different. We both had demanding jobs and weekends were important to both of us. I tried to fit in all the chores during the week after work so we had more free time together.

There was one Friday evening he came home, he was different – he wanted to get into bed immediately he arrived. It was lovely but there was something in his face saying I am a great lover, I am going to get you into bed and fuck you, not make love to you. I am a very perceptive person and I knew immediately that something different had happened that week. I was not thinking of this as we made love, it was later. I felt as if I did not know the truth behind him. I began to imagine he had been to bed with someone else and he was making a comparison. I just knew. His behaviour made me feel like that. Perhaps it affected the way I responded to him. Perhaps it affected the way he approached me. I may never know but it influenced our weekend relationship. I do not suppose many marriages would have survived the strain.

The pattern of our life with him working away carried on, but I was uneasy. He often went into his local office on a Saturday while I waited outside; he did not want me to go in. I had a feeling he was calling someone. Then he started having to return on a Sunday evening instead of Monday morning. He drank a lot more, he would lose weight and then put it back on again. I asked him if there was anything going on or a problem, but he said he was just working hard on a big job. Deep inside I trusted him implicitly; I trusted his love for me totally as I always had done. I had a demanding job myself which I had worked hard to get, and knew how it could dominate your thoughts over a weekend. So, I put some of his distance down to that. I made excuses for him.

Then one weekend we made love and it was uncomfortable – not painful but with a sort of stinging irritation. It did not feel right, and I thought it would go away before the next weekend. I was ignorant about these things. Then we saw he had a rash on his penis on and off. It took a few weeks of checking and discussion, but he finally went to the doctor and it turned out to be thrush, which he tried to convince me you could catch anywhere, or it just came. I wanted to believe him so much, I convinced myself I did, although I know I never really did. I suppose I was in denial. He had to use cream and they gave me suppositories. It cleared up but it left a kind of scar inside me mentally. Instead of the self-confidence and the sparkle I always had, there was a wariness in me, a sort of worm, wriggling its way around, casting doubts. I tried asking him if he had been unfaithful, but he denied it totally. I took his word for it.

It had to come out. I knew eventually when he did not come home for a bank holiday weekend. He told me he had to be at work and I just knew it was a lie. I had this weird dream about him and another woman. I even dreamt her name, which turned out to be correct. He rang me on the Saturday and said he had finished work and was going to a street party, something I know he would never do. He was in her house at the time and I knew it. If there had been a train that day I would have gone to check if I could find him, but something stopped me. I waited until the next weekend when he returned and asked him outright what was going on. He did not tell me straight away but eventually it all came out. He had been living with this woman for about six months, Monday to Friday. I really had not anticipated anything like that. I thought possibly a one-night stand. I knew things had not been as before because of the way he was treating me, but I could hardly take this in. He told me a bit about her and how he thought he was in love with her. It was like a dagger in my heart. I had had some funny phone calls while he was away, sometimes nobody spoke, and other times odd things were said. They now made sense. How could I have been so blind, so trusting of our love. I know now she was ringing to let me know, hoping it would lead to our breakup and him choosing her. Now I know his Saturday visits to the office were to call her. I had also found a set of keys I had never seen before; he said they were office keys, but I knew they were not. Maybe he had been leaving clues so I would find out and bring it to a head.

I was devastated, broken, my self-confidence vanished. The sparkle in my heart and eyes just faded. My father knew something was wrong when I saw him; he always spotted how I was, but I could not tell him, he was unwell, and he also thought so much of James. I did not want to destroy that, no matter what he had done. I still loved him, and I had to keep it to myself, if I could.

We talked a lot about it over the weekend, he still came home. During the weeks I felt like a zombie, I cannot even remember what went through my mind. I could not focus on what I was going to do. It got to a stage where he said he was going to pack everything in: me, his job, and his home. I could not believe it was what he really wanted. I had these terrible and strange feelings of wanting to injure myself. I wanted to crash my car into something. I wanted to put my hands on the kitchen hob and burn them. I felt I needed someone to care how much I was hurting. It was probably a cry for help. It turned out to be a silent cry. I did not injure myself or tell anyone. I tried to understand why. Sometimes I blamed not having children, sometimes I blamed the job, sometimes myself. I do not remember blaming James, perhaps I did. I wanted to hurt him and her, but above all I wanted him to love me again and not her. I believed he had stopped loving me. I know now he had not, I probably did then without realising but I was not thinking very logically during that period. We had not made love for a while – I did not want to while he was sleeping with someone else. I could not focus on whether we were going to split up or what would happen, but I was not prepared to accept the situation. I had more about me than that. I was often being asked out when he was away and always refused. Why couldn't he have done?

I found out all I could about her using someone I knew who lived in that town. I did not tell them why I needed to know but I learnt a lot.

We decided to have a short holiday together and try and sort things out in our minds. It was the worst holiday of my life. We went to Corfu, which did not impress me as I thought it would. Perhaps it was my frame of mind. It all went wrong. He hired a moped and nearly killed us falling off. I thought he was trying to get rid of me – that was one way to resolve things. I imagined he was telephoning her every time he was out of my sight. I was right.

I certainly did not feel like I had been on holiday when I returned. No decisions had been made. His job in that town was coming to an end in a few weeks. That weekend we sat and talked together, and I told him how I felt. I remember telling him how much I had loved him, and I had hoped we would grow old together. I think that day something persuaded him to stay with me, and he promised to give her up and never see her again. At that point I believed him.

I had loads of doubts; I think I could have coped with a fling while he was working away which he regretted and now wanted to be with me. I kept thinking if I had children would it have happened? Would it be the same? Now it is too late for me – I am too old for children.

He was still working away on and off but had changed to a different area, so I assumed he had put her out of his life as he said he had. I still could not get it out of my mind that he said he loved her. A few weeks later when he was at home, he was scratching his pubic hair; he said he had an itch. When we looked together, we saw he had crabs. I had heard of them but never seen them. I had no idea what to do and I felt sick. We shaved his hair and put disinfectant around and I did the same in case I had caught them from him in bed. I was physically sick, and I assumed that the woman he had been living with had given them to him. I insisted he went to the doctor. When he went, they gave him a test and he had a venereal disease called NSU, something non-specific. I then had to attend the clinic as someone he had slept with. I felt like a prostitute being examined and questioned. I had never had another partner and they looked at me as if they felt sorry for me. Although my tests were negative, they told me it could show up later in life and I had to go on a course of pills. They gave me terrible stomach pains, a rash and sickness but I took them, and I thought, I will never feel the same again. I could not believe James had done this to me. We had been married fifteen years, and been so in love and happy. Had he really changed towards me, or just taken what was on offer while he was away from home?

I had always had a high sex drive and enjoyed our love making, but I could not compare it to anyone else as James was the only man I had ever known as a lover. After those pills, it was not the same. I felt dry and uncomfortable, and I had lost my self-confidence and doubted that I was satisfying him sexually as a wife. Our lives and our relationship changed. I did not believe he was not still in contact with her. I found out the truth later. I also thought it was her that gave him the venereal disease. He told me the truth a long time later.

The truth was, or so he said, that he never told her he would not see her again, he just never contacted her again. He said he had a terrible conscience about it, which adversely affected our lives for the next few years because he felt guilty towards her. I think he blamed me. If only I had known the truth about his feelings, we may have avoided all the wasted and unhappy times that followed. Who knows now? He said the week after he decided he was just leaving, he went into a pub on his next job, met a woman, got drunk and slept with her and that was how he contracted the NSU.

I was obviously low at this point in my life. A friend asked me to go to a palmist with her, which I did. Funnily, it was a lady I met when in Corfu who recommended the lady we went to. It was an amazing experience. I will never forget. I am not a religious person, but I think there is something else we do not know about and will find out one day. I am very perceptive and often have dreams and/or know things before they happen. This lady talked about the past and present and she was so accurate, it was uncanny what she told me about myself and James. The past and present was so true, I had to believe what she told me about the future, although some of it I believed to be impossible. I would have to wait and see. She told me all that had happened, even names and what people looked like. She did tell me that he loved me but did not always show it. It was a small comfort.

Chapter 9
Too Young

We had met in the swinging '60s when one did not expect teenagers to be as naïve as me. James had quite a lot of experience with girls – I did not know that at the time. I suppose my background had made me what I was, although one would think it would be the opposite. I expect my father's strictness had a lot to do with it. Strangely though, the strength he had somehow got built into me and made me believe I knew things that I did not, a sort of false self-confidence. I eventually had to pay for that, but I would not change a lot if I had a choice, looking back. I might have at the time.

I had an older sister who did not like me much; I do not know why, just a personality clash. I remember her often calling me a baby, and poking or hitting me when no one was looking. My mother never seemed to notice when it happened, and my father was away in the Services after the war. Whenever he came home, I got lots of his attention as I was a sickly child. This made my mother and sister jealous, so I was not always treated fairly. I must have recognised this quite young because I always tried not to cry when my father left or my sister did something horrible. I think that is when a lifelong skill of covering up my feelings developed. It became a natural way for me to cope. I always seemed to get ill when my father was away, the sickly child of the family they called me, so I tried to stop telling them when I felt sick but somehow still ended up at the doctors and taking medicine that never tasted very nice, despite what they would tell you. I also developed a fear of doctors that would stay with me for the rest of my life. I do not remember what they did to treat me, but it must be in my subconscious somewhere. Maybe I have paid for that, or maybe I am healthier because I keep away from them.

Despite my sickly young childhood, I did well at school and unusually for someone of my background, passed the 11 Plus and went to grammar school. I did not want to go because all my friends were going to the local secondary modern. They called me the posh brain box who was going to the grammar. It was a girls-only school with only female teachers, again I think that is why I prefer mixed company to female gatherings. Strange how circumstances beyond your control shape the future of your inside self.

The first knowledge I gained about sex was from some of the girls relaying their experiences with boys they knew. When they told us, they asked if we had done it and they would only tell us if we said yes. I learnt to say yes even though I did not know what I was supposed to have done. One girl had a regular boyfriend and she told us one day how when he was saying goodnight, he took her knickers off. She said she got so wet it was running down her legs. I said I did not know it was raining last night and everyone laughed, so I did. It was a long time before I knew what the joke was. One girl related the details of her friend's abortion –an illegal one in those days. I did understand that and vowed no matter what happened I would never have one. I kept my views forever against abortion. They were strengthened because I had no children of my own, but they were formed before all that happened.

I met boys at the youth club and danced with them and fancied them, but I did not know quite what for. My father always had to know where I was when I was out, and who I was with. I had strict instructions on the time to be home and knew I would not be allowed out next day if I was late. A couple of boys tried to get further than a feel of the breasts, which I liked as it made me feel nice, but I never liked them enough to let the hand go further than the knicker elastic. I remember one boy trying it in the Sunday afternoon cinema to which a big group of us went together. All the boys were trying the same thing at the same time. It was a good film and I wanted to see it, so I stopped the boy going too far but I learnt about getting wet. I had been to a couple of parties where boys had kissed and cuddled me when the opportunity arose but I always said no; I felt I was saving myself for someone special. Although lots of my friends said they had lost their virginity, I was not tempted just for the sake of it. I was still not sure exactly what would happen.

We were both seventeen when I met James at the bus stop. I was smitten immediately but did not realise it for what it was, or what it meant at the time. I was too naïve. It was as if my heart expanded at first sight. I just wanted to hold his hand or be cuddled by him. After the first kiss, I wanted to be kissed even more. We just seemed to want to be together at every opportunity. I immediately neglected my girl friends, and just saw James.

I did not know that James already had a steady girlfriend. He did not tell me at the time, and he was two-timing her with me for a while. A leopard never changes his spots they say. It was his mother who let me know when I met her – she called me by a different name. I think she did it on purpose because she liked the other girlfriend. His mother got to like me eventually, but it took a while and she was disappointed I was not a Catholic – she wanted lots of grandchildren. Many years later, we told her James could not have children and she never said a word to me about it. I think at the outset James really liked something about me and like all young men in the sixties, wanted to get into my knickers asap. Just his touches made me melt at that time, and his goodnight kisses on the stairs up to my parents' flat could give me an orgasm. It was only a matter of weeks before I let him see and touch, but not go all the way. I wanted to but I suppose I was afraid of pregnancy in those days. A few months later, using condoms, I lost my virginity in a beach hut on the coast. I think by then James had given up his old girlfriend and we were both very much in love. We just seemed to belong together, and it was a mutual feeling. We had no money except our wages, which did not go far, but we enjoyed just being together, playing music, going to clubs, parties and even just hanging outside somewhere. We took chances and made love whenever we could, and I was frequently worried if my periods were late, but we both just enjoyed it so much. We were a typical sixties couple but not promiscuous, we were happy with each other. He would sometimes waylay me on my way to work and totally against my nature of responsibility, I would take the day off and spend it with him. We just did not want to be apart. I felt he was my one true love forever.

After two years together we got engaged. It took another two years, with two jobs each, to save for a deposit on a house. We got married and moved into our new home the next day; no money for a honeymoon. It always just felt right – we worked, we played, we furnished the home gradually. We were always poor, watching every penny, but we stayed happy. We just knew we would have children and live happily ever after. James was ambitious financially, having been an extremely poor child, and I supported him in that ambition and more by making a home for us and our future family, which I longed to have.

Our sex together was fantastic, although I had nothing to compare it with apart from what you read in books, or occasionally heard from other women. I never once turned him down as I loved it and wanted it as much as him. I had orgasms easily, they sometimes came too quick. I would often initiate sex by walking around in suspenders and boots, which he loved, sometimes just no knickers. It was an extremely healthy love life and I thought I was enough for him and satisfied him. He loved all sport, but I could even turn him on while he watched his favourite team play football on TV. He was put out if he missed seeing a goal, but it did not stop us. We were in love, and loved to make love. He would get me to go out without knickers on. If we went for a walk, he would always find a quiet spot in the woods or countryside to enjoy each other. We both loved it outdoors. I was so confident I was enough for him. I was not so naïve that I thought he would not be tempted by other women on offer while he worked away, but I thought our love was enough for him to be faithful. I was one hundred and ten percent confident. For my part I was often hit on by men at work or social things I attended on my own, and I did fancy some of the guys. They were usually strong, successful people, some even quite wealthy, but I really loved James so much I just did not contemplate cheating on him, even after he did it to me. It did cross my mind later when I was really suffering, but I knew it was not the answer and I would regret it. It would just be a fuck rather than the tender

loving moments we had shared. Just not for me.
I wrote him a poem to show how I felt.
Met at the bus stop
Went to a coffee shop
What a place to meet
Made my heartbeat
Knew that was the start
Of never wanting to part
You asked for a date
Must have been fate
That first goodnight kiss
And that feeling of bliss
You took me off on your scooter
My very first suitor
We went down to the coast
You bought Sunday roast
I couldn't hazard a guess
At the feel of your caress
It fluttered my heart
Never wanted to be apart
Got a valentine by post
I felt luckier than most
My life would be a mess
If I had to settle for someone less
It was like an expert casting
In a play everlasting
My heart was all a dither
Must never let it wither
Then came that band of gold
Any life alone was sold
There was a magnetic hold
We grew into one mould

Together we are bold
The story is nearly told
Life will never be cold
Even when we grow too old

I just did not think of problems and what might go wrong, we were just always optimistic. I did not get pregnant despite our love life which was healthy and enjoyable. We both had regular jobs and for the day, an income we could live on. We decided to sell the house and buy another one to cut down our travelling to work. When we moved and changed our doctor I went to be checked as to why I was not getting pregnant. They found no problem with me, so they did tests on James only to find he had a low sperm count and some sort of antibodies in his system. This was the early days of IVF and they offered further procedures, but we both wanted our own children and they said they could not use sperm from James. The thought of a stranger's child was not the same for me. I held on to the hope that a low sperm count was not a nil sperm count and perhaps we would still have our own children one day. I held onto that hope for years and years, and suppressed the maternal feelings inside. I used to knit and crochet baby clothes for all my friends who were pregnant, but I had to stop, it was too sad for me. I put my energies into a career at which I became successful, but it never compensated for what I really wanted. Our mutual love kept me strong and I never resented not having children, or felt sorry for myself. I accepted it was not meant to be, it was not James' fault. If I had James, it was enough. I did not contemplate the idea that I would end up without him or children.

James never really said how he felt about it. It did not seem to matter to him that we did not have children and I did not want to hurt him by bringing it up. He was more focussed on us being financially secure.

He put all his efforts into work and progressed well. As a result, he had to start working away from home quite a lot. I was not happy but did not want to hold him back. So, I just got on with it and worked on my career as well. He usually travelled with other colleagues, some single and some married. Some of them became our friends and he often brought single guys home to stay. I always welcomed them.

I did not think his love for me had changed because he could not have children, and I knew I loved him just as much as ever. I felt I was doing everything I could to support him in his career and his home life. I was enjoying my work as well and getting promoted. We had a good income and a happy life, and I believed we were a happy and contented couple. I kept any sadness to myself regarding a family. I loved him too much.

Life was good, and we were happy and successful. We had good friends, but we did lose contact with some of those who had children and moved away. We no longer seemed to have the same things in common. We moved home ourselves again so were not as near to our old friends. We were both extremely focused on our jobs, which carried a lot of responsibility and could be quite stressful in those days. We had to put lots of hours in, and often worked at home over the weekend on reports or other aspects of the job. Despite all this, we remained remarkably close and I had no doubts about our mutual love for each other.

Was I naive? Was I blind? Was I deceiving myself? Was I at fault? Had I wasted my life with him and denied myself children? I had to ask myself these questions. I did not get all the answers.

PART THREE
AFTER

Chapter 10
But

He was back home. The day after, I felt strange and strained. I should have felt good, but something was weighing me down. I think it came to light when we got in the bath together and started chatting again. He said how he had chosen to come back because he wanted to. He wanted us to try again and make our marriage work. But. There always seemed to be a 'but'. He had been looking forward, he said, to living on his own and having another way of life. I wondered if he was already having regrets. He said he wanted to be honest about it all. Then he told me how he had wanted to let her down lightly, and that he had told her if she wanted a chat to ring him. I was not going to accept this. I asked him if he was going to ring her. He said she had asked him to ring her over the weekend, but he told me he was not going to. I suddenly felt nothing had changed. I asked myself, should I have agreed so readily for him to come back? I knew it was right, we are meant to be together. I said I was not happy about any contact with her, he assured me there was nothing to worry about – there would be no sex, probably just a drink and lunch. He could not seem to see how I felt, it was as if it should not matter to me. I decided not to cover up my feelings. I said it was no good for him or me, or even for her wanting to cling on. I said either he or she was clinging on in the hope of more, and either he had chosen a marriage or not. Then he started shouting again about how I could not own him, and he was going to do what he wanted. I felt something collapse inside me. There was not any fight left but I said what I felt, and I think he finally appreciated where I stood. I did not want him back under those circumstances. I did not know what else to say or do, so I decided I would wait and see what he did. I did not want to keep talking in circles. I did wonder what sort of woman, knowing he had come back, still wanted to cling onto a married man in that way and knowingly destroy a marriage. She must know it could only cause hurt and harm; was she that desperate to keep him? I also knew it had been her frequently ringing up and hanging up when I answered, but I did not tell him. I told him that he might as well go and not prolong the pretence. He said that was not what he wanted. I let him stay, believing he really wanted it and would have no further contact with her. I knew I had no trust in that, but did not want to throw away probably the last chance to save our love if it was still a two-way feeling. I said to myself, why would he come and try if he did not want it back? He knows I will not accept sharing him with another woman.

We laid in the bath silently. Then he cuddled me and played with my breasts, and I felt drawn to him as I always had. However, again it was there between us and it was too soon – had he caught anything from her? I was not prepared to risk that again. He was sure he had nothing wrong, but I was not. From my perspective, he had to be checked out at the hospital before I could relax or even think about sex with him. He spoke about us making love again and made me feel as if I was going to be on trial; was he comparing me with his other experiences? It if worked things would be okay, he said, if it does not maybe it will be the end. I do not think he meant it like it sounded, but I took it that way and felt afraid. It was not the sort of feeling and thought I should have when trying to repair a relationship. I hoped desperately that I could overcome it. Maybe I should not have agreed so readily for him to come back after those months alone. I had so many doubts.

I seemed to be, and live, in a sort of trance; everything just carried on, but I was not totally aware or involved in what was around me.

I wanted desperately to trust him, more than anything, like I used to. I wanted to believe all he said. I should not have done. She rang him and he met her; he had told me he would tell me if it happened. She rang and told me. What did she hope that would achieve? When I asked a few days later because he had not said anything, he twisted it and said he had told me he would tell me if I asked. I had tried not to ask because I had believed he would tell me. He said he had met her and told her it was over and that he would not be ringing her but, another but, if she wanted to ring him, she could. I could not understand why he could not finish it all – did she mean so much to him? I told him again it was not acceptable to me, it would be coming between us and there was no chance for us with her clinging on to him. I did not mention her calling and telling me because I thought that was what she wanted. We got back again to him wanting the freedom to do what he wanted, when he wanted, with whom he wanted. I said if things have not changed, he does not want a marriage and he should not have come back. I told him to piss off back to her, his flat or his other life he wanted. Why had he bothered to come back to me? We went over it all again that evening and something inside me snapped; it all felt so useless. I thought I could never trust him again or believe a word he said. I felt he did not want to give her up, and really enjoyed being with and seeing her. I felt he was playing a game with me, coming back to see how long I would put up with it, believing I would have him back at any price. He was wrong. He kept saying he just wanted to let her down lightly and slowly. I was not thinking rationally, I was exhausted, exasperated and devastated. I threatened to kill myself to solve his dilemma; I even got a knife out to cut my wrists. I just felt useless, hurt, wasted, used and as if my feelings meant nothing to him, and never would again. I thought I had been hurt as much as possible by him, but this seemed to add to the wounds already there. They were so fresh they reopened, and it was as if they were being dug into with something to see how far it would go in. I became a bit hysterical and he seemed to care again and said I would get what I wanted. He told me he had just intended to see her as a friend and let it die out. I did not think he wanted it to die out. She must know what trouble it would cause for me still knowing she was around. How can a woman not want it to end when she knows it is over between them? She would respect herself more if she did accept it, but she is not that type of person. He eventually said he would tell her when she rang that he would not be seeing her again. But he added again, it would have been better if I had let him do it in his own time, as if I had ordered him to do it. I had not done, but I had told him how I felt and what he was proposing was not acceptable to me. I did not think I was being unreasonable, he did. I was afraid now we were going to go backwards, and he would make me pay for him giving her up – the price if he wanted me as his wife. I did not want it to be like that. I really wanted him to care enough about me that he did not want to see her. At that moment he did not, but he said he was prepared to give her up for me, reluctantly. I thought maybe he still loved me, but I was not sure. I said he should not have asked to come back if he still wanted her in his life, that he was trying to use me and lying by omission. Why had he come back under those circumstances? Did he really think I would not find out, or that she would not let me know in the hope of keeping him?

I still wanted to believe and trust him, give him his freedom that he kept on about, which if it was time on his own, I was happy to do. He kept repeating he should be able to do what he wanted, when and with whom. Could he really expect me to be happy about that; what had changed, why had he come back?

I asked myself how long I was going to let this trial, as I saw it, carry on and could not yet decide. I asked what he wanted from me. He said just get yourself right, whatever that meant.

I had been trying for so long. I did not know what else to do. He said he wanted me to be happy, not relying on him to do things. He said I always wanted him to do the things, like answering the door or phone and talking to people. It was true because if I did it, he would criticise what I said or did. It was not because I could not do it. I thought he wanted to be the man. Why did he not realise what I had coped with alone when he was not there for weeks on end, away working? I did everything. How did he think I had achieved so much at work and reached the position I now had if I was afraid to do things for myself? I am, and have always been, a very capable lady. My weakness being in love.

I could not decide what I should do next to try and make

things work. I had decided to give it a go, despite my reservations. I decided I would try and get some out of the house activities going, make a concerted effort, perhaps with playing squash or learning and improving my French. My mind kept going back to wondering what he was doing when I am out – could I trust him? I really wanted to have confidence in him again and believe what he said, but it was just not there. I wondered if it ever could be again. I hoped he would give it a chance to come back. I was not sure whether to pretend all was okay with me, or tell him my doubts.

The weekends came; around our workdays, that was when we generally talked a bit. I was still extremely low and felt under tremendous pressure not to get him doing something he did not want to do. He thought he knew how I felt, but I believe he did not have a clue. I felt I was wasting my time trying to be what he wanted, do what he wanted, be what I wanted, do what I wanted. Nothing seemed to make him feel about me. He seemed already to resent his time being spent with me. I got evasive half answers to any questions I asked or suggestions I made of things to do. It seemed as if he was determined for things to remain as they were, and all the effort was coming from me. I could feel myself paying for it all again, being punished because he had given up what he called his freedom, and was blaming me. It still seemed to be about her, although he said it never was. He still said he had enjoyed being with her, and would have liked to continue until he was ready to finish it when and how he wanted. I could not understand why he should not see or feel what I was going through, and how much it was hurting me. I would eventually get to sleep at night after trying for hours to put it all out of my mind, but it kept coming back. I would then wake up after a few hours and all that would be in my mind was him with her in bed, in the pub, in the sports club, in his car. All the things I had found out they had been doing together. The fact that he said he was not bothered if he never saw her again, did not sink in. He was showing me different – he appeared to be pining after something, or someone, and I assumed it was her. I felt more and more useless. I was putting a lot of energy into keeping my job going, in which I knew I had been letting myself down. I was putting effort into thinking about us and trying not to think about her, and the anonymous calls that still came. It was all taking a lot out of me. I could not see anything coming from James to help me. He kept telling me to be positive and get myself right. Why could he not give me just a little help? When I mentioned helping me he said, I am back, you were desperate for that. It is better than if I was not here isn't it? I had already my doubts about that, although deep down I knew we were better together. Instead of things improving, I felt further destruction of myself. I thought I was coping until he came back; it was the wrong thing for me. Oh, how I tried; perhaps it did not show to him, or perhaps he did not want to see it. There were the odd moments of him appearing to care, but nothing real; perhaps I did not appreciate how much he had suffered or been hurt; maybe he was trying to get himself right and using all his energy, so not much was left for us. Perhaps it would come later? Was it wishful thinking on my part? Was I kidding myself?

How can you want to do something so badly and not have a clue where to start? Decide on action and take it – how many times can you do that with no results, over and over again? How often, or for how long, could one continue like that? I had started to feel I needed to smash up everything around me, including myself. I think it was just total frustration in more ways than one.

I had not had any sex for about six months. I thought back to how fruity he used to make me feel, and wondered if it could ever happen again. He still had not had a check-up with the doctor and I was afraid it would all go wrong. I had to suppress those thoughts, or it would be bound to fail. I still had not told a soul. In some ways, I was proud I had not used anybody, glad I had not. In other ways, perhaps I could have got some advice, support, ideas that would have improved things. I doubt it really. I like to make my own decisions. I am not always right, but mostly I have taken the right path. Despite James' contrary suggestions, I have always been independent and self-sufficient.

I got another phone call at work, which upset me and this time I told James about it; I got angry about it, partly because James did not seem to believe me. He then later said he asked her about it, and she denied making it. I said, you are still contacting her then, you'd better leave. He believed her rather than me and then seemed to accuse me of ringing her. I answered the phone early one morning and someone asked for her by name. I asked who and they repeated it. I asked what number they wanted, they repeated the name and hung up. I recognised her voice and accent and I am sure it was her, knowing that we would still be under pressure and trying to make things go wrong. I had known girls at work do things like that, completely out of character, because they had split up with someone and were hurting. He seemed to side with her and said, adamantly, that it could not have been her. He asked me again if I had ever rung her. I certainly did not want to speak to her, hear her or have anything to do with her. I think she must have been telling him I was ringing her when she was ringing me. I knew where she worked and her home address; I felt like going and confronting her, but felt she would have won something if I did that.

I did not believe his assurances that he was not still in some sort of contact with her. If that was the case, what was he doing with me? There is no way I will accept it. There is no way we can get back to a proper married life with that between us. What does he want for the two of us? Does he think I will finally agree to a compromise? There is no way. How long can I give this trial?

Chapter 11
Trial Run

I was so afraid he was going to start up with her again and try to keep it from me. I am not sure why I felt like that. I think it was his attitude. He seemed to still blame me for stopping him seeing her. I suppose he was right, but I had never asked him to come back, just told him how I felt about it and that I could never accept it with her, or anyone else. He seemed to think that because he said he would not have sex with her any more, that it would be okay. Could he not understand my feelings? It was as if he wanted to rub salt into the wounds, and make me pay for us getting back together again. He said when he was away, he wanted us to be together – why did he not feel like that now when we are together? I just could not understand his attitude; I tried to get him to explain but I never got an answer. Maybe one day I would get to know. How much time would we have? I felt as if I was on trial. If I could not make him feel better towards me, we would have to go through it all again. I knew I would not survive as well if that happened. I was not even sure yet that I had survived this time. I did not seem to know myself. I could not do the things I wanted to do. I felt suppressed and trapped – a useless failure at my marriage. Surely, I had something more to offer? I had lost myself. I could not give up on us now – this was my last try, I knew that. I needed to get back some inner strength that had got me through life's traumas successfully before. None like this.

The next night's dream was not so much like a nightmare. I dreamt that he finally realised that she was doing him harm. She had been telling people anonymously at work what he had been doing with her, and hinting at security risks with his job. She had rung his boss and his colleagues. I know it was only a dream and hoped it would not come true. When he found out, he finally told me he had no regrets about giving her up, and it was as if we had both been released and could make our lives work together again. When I got up I felt better than for ages; it seemed silly to let a dream affect your life so much, but so many of mine had influenced my life next day by coming true that I was optimistic. I know many dreams do not come true but maybe half of this one would. I would need to wait and see.

Later, we started talking again; he asked me how I felt. I said okay, although I did not. I was trying to and felt better than the day before. He said he felt numb when I asked him what he felt about things. There was an overlong pause, and he went back again to how he had been looking forward to a different way of life. I was getting sick of hearing this. He said how he would have enjoyed it, how when two people met with their own set up, not demanding anything of the other, it was different. That is how it is when most people meet, why could he not see that? He said he did and had chosen to come back because thinking of me would have spoiled his life, which was going to be totally devoted to pleasure. Then he said again, I am back, what more do you want, as if he was doing me a great favour. He seemed to forget all the time that I had asked him to leave because he had another woman in tow. I told him I did not want him with me under just any conditions and that if it all happened again, I would do the same thing and there would be no coming back. If that is what he wants, he may as well leave now. He said, I wish you were that tough all the time and I would know where I stood. I felt anything but tough and I was sad, but I did not really want him to say that in case it led to more arguments. Well I called them discussions, he called them arguments.

I realised how unbalanced I was about it all one day; I rang him at about twelve-twenty just to wish him luck at the dentist. I had felt low all morning and felt physically sick. I do not know what made me feel like that, I was not actually sick, but I felt as if I was going to be. His office said he had gone out for lunch and some fresh air. I just assumed he had gone to meet her again, despite all he had told me. I just crumpled inside – all the pains and hurt came back. It was nearly as bad as I had felt at the beginning. Luckily, I had already had a sandwich – I could not have eaten. I did not go to lunch, I did not work, I just sat there in a dreadful state not knowing what to do. I thought of going over and checking on him, but knew I would not do that and, anyway, I would probably miss him. I thought of challenging him about it that night and if it was true, telling him I never wanted to see him again. I did not know how I could do that but, as he had always said, I would cut off my nose to spite my face. He was right and often I could not help myself. I tried not to, but I rang him again just before two and they said he was still at lunch. I guessed he would then go straight to the dentist. I nearly went home sick, I was in such a state, but knew if I told anyone I was going I would have burst into tears. I stuck it out, just looking at papers on my desk, doing nothing. Then he rang me at four and told me he had met a friend called Terry, and gone to his club near the dentist. I had no reason not to believe him. He was in a rush so I had no time to say much about anything, which was probably a good thing or he would have sensed how I felt. I could not unwind or calm down. I left work early and just went for a drive, I am not sure where. I ended up in a traffic jam in the rush hour and got home about seven. I knew he had an evening meeting to attend, so I just wanted to get myself right before he came home. I did not know where to start. I felt on the verge of a breakdown, if one can feel that in advance. Please do not let this happen, I said to myself. Learn a lesson and start to trust him again; I did not know if I could. I knew I wanted to; I wanted a lot from myself and something from him that I did not seem to be getting yet. Please, please come back, let us be friends and lovers again, man and wife. I knew it was possible if the two of us wanted it. I was not sure yet if we both did.

I think the evening before had affected me more than I realised, even though it ended on a happy note. I felt so unsure of everything. We had agreed to go to the cinema near his office. We were to meet at the Tube station at five-thirty. I was early as usual; it was cold so I thought I would walk towards his office as far as the roundabout, then turn back so that I did not miss him. He came around the corner as I was about to turn around; I waved and smiled, he just looked irritated and pissed off with me. He pecked me on the lips and said he thought we were going to meet at the Tube station. I explained I was early and decided to walk, but he just gave me a horrible look and walked off towards the cinema. I literally tagged along trying to keep up. At one point he told me to hurry up. I told him he did not seem happy to see me; he said he had a hard day, but it was not that kind of look. I felt devastated inside again, he just appeared not to want to be with me. I guessed he resented meeting me and not her. I imagined perhaps he had taken her to the cinema and was now missing her company, and did not want me with him. I wondered why on earth he had come back to me if he was going to do this. I attempted to keep myself cheerful, but it was impossible with his attitude, the way he spoke to me and looked at me. When we arrived at the cinema, we were too early to pick up the tickets; I suggested a walk around, but he just ignored me and sat down. I had to go to the toilet so as not to break down and shout at him, or do something. Was he trying to make me not want him, I said to myself? I calmed down a bit in the loo and suggested a drink when I came out; he said he did not want one and he then suggested a walk. This time we went; I tried to explain how I felt and asked what the problem was. He told me he did not like me lurking around his office and that was why he was annoyed. I wondered if he was ashamed of me, or did he have something to hide? The walk seemed to cheer him up a bit, so we went back for the tickets and had a drink before the film. The film was good and cheered us both up. When we came out, he semi-apologised, and I tried to get him to understand how I felt when he behaved like that. I said he had chosen to come back, he had a choice, why was he not making the most of it and trying to make it work rather than living with regrets? He did not deny that was the case and said he agreed. He cuddled me on the way back to the car, and seemed like a different person when he looked at me and spoke. More like the old James I had loved so much. I did not know where I really stood, which side of him was the truth. Could he be trying a total con on me for some ulterior motive? Could it be related to our finances – I would have to be careful. I had not mentioned my plans for a mortgage of my own and buying him out. I had sorted this out and I could do it. That kind of trust was not in me. Had he gone back to how things were, seeing her when he could and keeping it from me? All sorts of things went through my mind. I suppose anyone would feel uncertain and insecure in my position. I didn't know what to do – one minute I wanted to hit him and walk away, the next I wanted to hold him so tight he could feel my love go into him, perhaps give a little back. There was no way of stopping myself loving him – that was the one thing I was sure of. Could I bear this to carry on and stand up to it for much longer? I did not think so; I did not know, but I had to give it a try. They say love conquers all, but to do that it has to flow both ways. I knew he still loved me, but I am not sure he still wants to. Maybe he is trying to stop. I hope not for his sake as much as my own. I believe he would never like himself again. I hope I am not wrong about our special feelings for each other. A once in a lifetime, too good to throw away.

I tried so hard to get myself on top of things, but it did not seem to work. On the surface it did for small periods of time, but inside I felt destroyed. As soon as things were a little better, everything that he had said and done would take over my mind. When I told James I was low he just said, sort yourself out. Think of how much you wanted me back when I was not here. I said things had not changed, but I did not, and never did, want him back under any circumstances. If he had other women, I did not want to share my life with him and never would.

I would be trying to get on with my work, my job had really suffered; it was only because I had worked so hard for years that I do not think anyone contemplated that I could have sat all day and done virtually nothing. If something was not finished, they assumed I was too busy with something else.

I did try, and if it came into my mind that he was still going to see her at lunchtime, I would try and shut it out. He said she had not rung, and he had not seen her, but something stopped me believing him. I think I felt she was going to accidently, or on purpose, bang into him in the street and he would take her for a drink or something. He appeared to me as if he wanted to see her again – he did not say he did not. Maybe just to prove to himself I could not tell him what he could or could not do. What he did not realise was that if he did see her, he would no longer have the choice of me – that I had decided, and I would not go back on it. No matter what it cost me, that was my decision for my own sake. He would again say, cutting off your nose to spite your face, but it would not be that – it would be cutting out my heart to save the rest of my body; could one survive that? No matter how hard I fought against it, thoughts of her kept creeping into my brain no matter whether I was asleep, awake, reading, thinking, or working. I had the feeling she was like a leech where he was concerned. She did not have the guts to let go when she knew she was being flicked off. Then the doubt would come back – perhaps he had not flicked hard enough, perhaps I was just imagining it all, but how was I to know the truth? I wished I could believe what he said but he often looked to be contemptuous of me and bored at being with me, as if he was still longing for something else. Either he wanted me as his wife or not; why could he not make up his mind and put some effort in that I could feel? If I brought it up, he would say again I am here, as if that was all that mattered. When would things get right again? I had so much love for him, but was still having to hold a lot of it back. Perhaps things will change if he gets his promotion; maybe it would just put him under more pressure. He had just applied for a more senior job. I really wanted him to get it as I always wanted him to get on and achieve what he was aiming for. I still had this feeling someone may have tried to sabotage his chances of getting the job by mentioning her. Affairs at work could affect promotions in those days. The doubts were always there; how could I be more positive and banish them? I would probably feel better if he would go to the hospital, but he kept saying he had not had the time and, anyway, he knew he did not have anything wrong with him, but he would go eventually. Why did he not see how important it was to me? If the roles were reversed, he would not be happy about getting close to me physically. I explained how it was coming between us and he said he would go when he was ready. At the back of my mind I wondered if he was still considering sex with her. Was that why he was waiting?

One morning, he kissed my breasts and held me close. I think if he had really tried and progressed, I would have given in and made love. But he just kissed and held me close. It felt so good. It made me remember and think of when my happiness just made me sparkle inside. My eyes used to feel alive, glittering, full of love and contentment. Not every minute of every day but generally, even when James was not with me. The feelings I had for him, and knew he had for me, were felt in everything I did. When did it go, I wondered, and could it come back? Even when I forced my eyes to smile, the feelings were not there and it did not appear outwardly as it used to. I used to see it in his eyes too. Happiness with me, love for me, good feelings about what we had achieved together and what we would do in the future. That is not what I saw in his eyes now. Would I again, and what could I do to help him and me, and us, get it back? We still had so much, but there were a lot of other things trying to destroy it and stop it being there again. I am sure we both want it. I would love to feel my sparkle back, not a false forced one for a few minutes, but the real one. I am sure it is still inside me, just suppressed. Just thinking of him when he is not there with me, tells me it is there, just waiting to be able to come back to the surface. I hope he has these feelings too. I had tried not to love James, but it had not worked.

Chapter 12
Doubts

I could not remember when I had last been lifted so much. Just hearing he had got the job. Even though I had been 99.9% sure that he would get it, I had the little sabotage doubts. I was so excited for him. I sort of swelled inside with happiness and pride for him. I knew how much he wanted it. He was not in the office when I rang to tell him how pleased I was. I wanted to go round to him and kiss and hug him and tell him how I felt about it, and how proud I was of him. I drove home feeling good; when I arrived, I did not know what to do; I was on a high. I put some champagne into the fridge, hoping we would drink to his new job later after he had played his usual game of squash. I was delighted when he arrived; we hugged and kissed; he was incredibly pleased, but not as full of it as I had expected. I was so happy for him. We ate together and he went off to play squash. I still could not settle, probably because I needed to do something to unwind and it is difficult alone when you are high because of someone else. I got the champagne and glasses ready for when he arrived; he appeared pleased and we toasted together, and sat and had a drink. We started chatting about the job. I do not know when things changed between us. I told him I had known he would get the job as I sometimes knew other things in advance. I remember him saying, you do not know everything, in an odd sort of way as if he was keeping something from me. He probably did not mean it in that way, but it really hurt. I started fishing a bit to see who had rung, and congratulated him. I did not want her to have any part of his success or celebrations. He told me his department may be moving its office, along with some of the other departments. I immediately wondered if her department would be going as well. He did not know I knew where she worked and what she did, but I did not say anything. Then he told me what his new job would entail, and it seemed to relate to work she was involved in as well, in my mind anyway. I was still very insecure and vulnerable, although much stronger. Anyway, I asked him, he said he did not know, in any case he did not come across her in his work role. I told him then I could not yet really trust him and/or believe everything he said, even though I wanted to. He asked what I thought he was doing, and I said he often disappeared for the odd half hour or so and he could be meeting her, even though he said he was not. He got a bit annoyed and said he was not going to check with me before he went for a walk, and he was going to do what he wanted. I really did not want to spoil what was a celebration, so I tried to explain it was just how I felt, and I was still really hurting again at the things he had said. I asked if he would like his new job with the other life he kept saying he wanted, and he said yes in a roundabout way, but that he had to choose and he had chosen me. I asked if it had all made him feel happier because he said he had gone looking for someone because he needed something in his life at that time. He looked up at the ceiling, as he often did when he was not going to tell me all the answers, and said, yes. Why could he not see how it all affected me, knowing he had no regrets and would do it all again apart from letting me find out, if he could help it. I did not see how I could get my trust of him back, knowing he felt like that. We went to bed and I tried not to let him see that I was crying, but he did. We were both sorry it had come up and spoiled the celebration. I did not sleep much again. He was nice to me in the morning, and I said sorry. He said he understood, but I do not think he did concerning my hurt inside. I never felt well any more. I did not look well either. I had even fainted one night and very nearly on several other occasions, but he did not show much concern.

The next day I still felt up because of his success; perhaps it would give him the challenge he needs in his life. I knew he would become even more successful, but I never wanted to tell him all I knew. I suppose there was still a lot of doubt about some things I still did not believe would ever happen, although I had a few more years to wonder. I had not told him some of the things I foresaw and what the palmist had told me.

I wanted to feel I had helped him to get the job with my encouragement in the past. I know it was down to James, but I wanted him to tell me I had helped. He did in a way, when I asked, but not in the way he once did when either of us succeeded with something. He was more into how special he is now. He had always been special to me and always would be. I wish I could be as special to him as I once was. That together specialness was still there underneath but when would it come to the surface again? Surely our love for each other could raise it again? We did love each other no matter what. I must try, but in order to do things he wants of me I needed to suppress my feelings again, particularly the ones of distrust, until they go. I will try. I am sure it is worth it. Please let him try to help me a little as well. I really need some from him, but again I am covering up most of that. I do not want him to think

I am needy.

It was weird the way I felt – one minute I would feel and believe he was really wanting things to be right again. I would not know what triggered it, but I would be right in the middle of something and a sort of depression would come over me, and totally stop me doing and concentrating on whatever I had been in the middle of. It was as if I was being warned that things were not quite right. I began to wonder if he was deceiving me again, making a great cover up effort and sneakily still seeing this woman, perhaps just like a friend like he said he had wanted. When I was at work, I would get these feelings he was with her. Whenever I rang him with these feelings he was not in the office. This made me doubt him even more. Then he would ring and say that he had been at a meeting or something, and I would feel terrible about the things I had thought. I no longer knew whether to trust the things that came into my mind, as I used to be able to. He did not help my doubts with the way he reacted to things. He bought an evening paper one night, which was rare, and I asked him where he bought it because I knew he did not pass a news stand when he had his car. Nothing suspicious had gone through my mind until he reacted that I was checking up on him and what did it matter where he got it? He said he wanted one especially for something and went out of his way to get it. It did not ring true somehow and then I naturally thought he had met her before he came home, but I did not say so in case I was wrong. I would only tackle him with the facts when I had them. I had to be sure.

Next day, he was on about going on holiday on his own. I had already had vivid dreams of him going to the South of France for a few days, having planned it when she would be there on holiday. The places and how they had planned to meet, were still clear in my mind even though I knew I only dreamt it. I do not know what I would do or how I would cope, if he really decided to go now. I would have to find out, somehow, the truth. If he was trying to mess things up. I had the number of a contact who could check what he was doing and where she was. If I had the proof that he was still seeing her, that would be the end. While there were still doubts, he was getting the benefit of my doubts with a little trust. My dreams can be wrong. I had got better at work. I was not totally down and unable to concentrate most of the day. I had some good periods where I would make progress in catching up on the things I had let go, but I still was not on top and my job was pretty demanding a lot of the time. There was never any doubt that I loved James and always would, but I had my doubts as to whether I would totally trust and believe in him again. I wanted to more than anything, and wondered if I could check on him to see if my doubts were unfounded in the hope that I would hate myself for it, as I believed I would no matter what the outcome. I knew I did not really want to do anything like that, say a private investigator, and hoped it would not come to it. Perhaps the periods of bad feelings would diminish if I waited a bit. I just do not know. I can say that when I am not full of doubts. When they are there, I would do anything to know for sure one way or the other. No matter how much I love him, I know that if he is at it again, it is the end of us. I would not give it another chance. Cut off my nose to spite my face, I suppose, but you cannot live and give for hope alone indefinitely. I still had doubts about everything – hopefully it would never arise – the thought of us giving up and ending breaks me up inside. Please do not let me have to go through all that again. Why do I get these emotions of doubt all the time; why can't I feel what he says is totally true, I do not know? I think it is the distance I feel he is keeping from me. We have not really got close again yet. Maybe if he went to the hospital things might change. I know he will go in the end, but why is he waiting so long – more doubts?

I suddenly realised, I do not know what I thought about it, I do not know what made me realise, but I know I could never love anyone else. I was incapable. Also, I would never let anyone else love me. They could try if it arose, but I would always have to let them know I did not want it. I also knew that loving and fucking had nothing in common. One day, though not yet, if it came to it, I could let someone fuck me and me fuck them, I think, but never love. I was desperate for both. If the love did not come from James, I would never have it again. I had been fucked by James as well as loved, but not for a long time. Why I suddenly felt this I did not know. Something had suddenly changed; it was overnight from James. How could he lift me so much? He said he felt better because he saw me looking better. Maybe I did, I tried but I certainly had not felt it. I must just have been covering it all up much better. It was one Thursday morning; I woke up and felt better. I had a feeling something had changed. James gave something to me again that morning, perhaps with a look or a touch, I do not know but I felt it.

Chapter 13
Destruction

I always had an inner strength, but I began to wonder if I had only had it because I had been loved. I really needed something from him that was not there. It had come back a little from him and at times I felt I was his again, but I was so unsure of him I could no longer share everything with him. I believed I had to keep some part of me to myself even though it was against my natural feelings. I was still so up and down, and it was not just his moods that made me that way. Although he still sometimes seemed miles away, it was not the same way he had been for so long, like distant. I think I was afraid it would not last, or that he was totally pretending, or that he had made up his mind he had been wrong to tell me so much and that things had not changed, but he was going to convince me they had. I think the dreams did not help; they were all similar. I would be hurting him in some way after we had split up. A bad one was when he was taking someone else to a dinner/dance where all our joint friends would be, and I agreed to go on another table without him knowing. I was with a really flash rich bloke, the tall dark handsome sort, which I would never choose. The guy was attentive and making sure I was happy and laughing. Everyone on James' table came and said hello and asked how I was. I chatted to them and pretended I was happy, and asked them how they were. The woman with him looked really put out and so did James. Eventually, he came and said hello and asked how I was; I said okay, a lie; I did not ask how he was. The woman with him was seething and I was glad. I could tell he did not care about her. I looked superb; I had made a great effort and shone. Something that would only happen in a dream. But it worked, he wanted me, and I wanted him, but I was not allowed to let it show. When he asked me to dance, I did not get a chance to reply; my partner came and whisked me away. I had hurt him but not as much as I had hurt myself. I did not even really want to be there. I woke up feeling awful. I knew I could not really do something like that and when you tell it as a dream, it sounds stupid but when you really believe it is happening, the hurt is unbearable.

I felt him get warmer towards me gradually, but still something inside was afraid to relax and accept and believe. I did not know what to do about it; I tried to say, trust until proven wrong, but I had already done that. I tried to convince myself if I believed him, I would feel better, and it worked. Then I would feel that depression come over me and I would doubt everything. Then I would feel him care and see his love, and I would relax again. I wish I knew what I needed. Perhaps if he went to the hospital and got cleared, it would be better. Why did he not make time and go? Did he not want to make love to me? I know he was under pressure at work but was sure he could have gone if he really wanted to. I began to wonder why he was putting it off, thinking there must be a reason. Perhaps he was hoping for a bit more on the side before he got checked out. I did not really believe that, but things he said just put doubts in my mind. I would just have to wait and see. I knew I would not be relaxed until he had been. It did not cross my mind that they would find anything wrong, until I thought maybe the reason he will not go is because he is afraid. I tried to stop thinking about it because there was nothing I could do about it. I had told him how I felt – it was up to him if he wanted to sort it.

I blew up one night, it was so stupid, and I do not know how it happened. He showed me a letter telling him about his raise in salary. It was from the building she worked in. That was where the personnel office was. I imagined her looking at his personal file and knowing so much about him. It just stung me inside as if I had swallowed a wasp and it waited until it reached my heart to sting me. I tried to control it but some of my feelings showed and he kept asking what was wrong. He could see something was wrong, but he did nothing to help me. I let it out and I swore, and I cried, then controlled myself and covered it up again. I upset him and ruined yet another weekend, and it was the last thing I had wanted. How could something so stupid cause so much pain? I suppose it was already there still waiting to be brought to life, not yet faded. I wished I could rub it out and perhaps start making him happy again. I wish I knew how. I could tell he was not happy. He said it was because I was unhappy. It was like a vicious circle and I could not see how to get us back in the middle, instead of going around the outside. We had been there many a time and I would keep trying; when I said that to myself, I felt I had not really tried much or awfully hard lately. It was not because I did not want to but something was holding me back. James knew and I knew, perhaps the outstanding hospital visit, but I was not sure that was all. Perhaps the pains I still felt. Keep fighting, I said to myself, that is what my father would have told me. If you want something, it is worth fighting for. I wondered deep down inside if really I did not want him any longer, but just the wondering at something like that tore at my heart so I knew I was wrong and still loved him so very very much. I felt sorry I had not given more to him recently and I really wanted to. I wanted to tell him that as well, but did not know if I could. I had this feeling that I must not suffocate him with my love for him and need of him. I did not want him to feel chained again – that is what I thought it might do. I was not sure what he wanted from me in that way anymore. I felt he wanted to make love to me again but then wondered if that was because he was not getting it elsewhere now, or perhaps because he knew I would not give myself to him until he had been to the hospital.

He finally went to the hospital and was told there was nothing wrong, which I think I knew anyway but wanted confirmation. He did not have the AIDS test – they only did that, apparently, on request. I should have felt something. I thought I should be elated or relieved, but I did not seem to feel anything apart from glad that I did not have to bring it up again. Maybe I was afraid that now we could make love and it would not be as good for him as with other people. I am not sure, but I think I had a worry of some sort of failure. Our love making had always been so good, I thought.

The day he went to the hospital, he also came home and said he had decided not to stay away from home the next night. It made me wonder why; he said he had done it for me as he knew I was worried about him going away. I had not been up to that point, although I had never really liked him being away. It was part of his job and I never tried to stop him because I did not want to hold him back for any reason in his job. I never told him I hated it. He gave me the impression he had made some decisions that day and had chosen some sort of compromise. Up till then I had not doubted he was doing what he said and going to a conference to listen to a presentation he would have to give in the future. It had come up over the weekend when he said he was taking his car and I asked if he was giving the other guy a lift, and he blew up again and accused me of checking on him. I thought this does not ring true, he is taking an afternoon off to do what. Why have things changed? He said he had decided for me, but I felt there was more to it than that. Maybe I would never know. I would see what he was like when he came home; perhaps it would put my mind at rest when I saw him. I was just showing an interest. When he then said he was going by train and would be home by nine o'clock I thought, what if he now rings and says he has missed the train or something? Was he saying some sort of goodbye to her he had not done already; I felt suspicious but had no proof he was lying? Luckily, I was out that evening; I needed something to take my mind off the thoughts that kept coming into it. I did not believe them, but they kept coming and plaguing me and I could not seem to do anything about it. All it seemed to do was cause destruction inside me. I would have to fight it even harder if things were ever to come right. Then I would wonder if I should check it all out, make sure the thoughts were not the truth. I would be better knowing, than doubting and wondering forever. I had done some research on getting a private detective, but they are expensive.

Chapter 14
Brick Walls

He has been different towards me recently –like a different person, more as he used to be. He seemed to care about me and how I felt. There was still something missing though – it was as if he really did not want to spend too much time with me. He was doing it because he thought he should. Perhaps that was unfair; I think he wanted to be with me but not for too long. It was as if he had to get away. But there were also times he made me feel good about us again. I even looked a bit better. I did not keep getting comments about looking so tired and worn out from everybody, which usually made me feel worse. I really thought things were coming right inside me, then I suddenly had an awful day. It did not cross my mind he was like this because he felt guilty.

He told me he was off to play squash after work that night and at first, I thought nothing of it. He mentioned it a couple of times and then made some other comments about how he would probably go for a drink after, so would have a bite with the blokes in the pub and would not need dinner with me. It did not concern me at that point, but I wondered if he wanted me to pick him up after. He was out all that day so did not go into the office; he kept telling me his movements for the day. I do not know what it was, but it seemed he wanted to reassure me about what he was doing. I suppose it made me suspicious.

I got low that day, back to being unable to concentrate on my work. I decided I would go across and watch him go into the squash courts. It was not to catch him out, but to prove to myself how stupid and untrustworthy I was being. I thought it would stop me from imagining things if I proved to myself that was all he was doing. I could not make up my mind whether to go. I wanted to and I did not. I think I had decided just to drive past at about the time he would go in, when he rang me. He was nice on the phone and said he would eat with me when he got home and why not have a glass of something with it? I felt guilty at how I had felt and decided to go home and forget it. Then I thought, why is he changing his plans, what is happening, has he still been seeing her and breaking it off slowly as he wanted? I did not suspect him of sleeping with her as he had been to the hospital. Perhaps he was seeing her for a drink as a friend; maybe he is finishing it still. I could not get rid of the feeling that there was something not ringing true about this evening. I went home anyway and got the food ready and put wine in the fridge. I hated coming into an empty house, it seemed hard to conquer my feelings as I entered alone. I no longer had that joyous feeling of arriving home. I often had to force myself not to drive off elsewhere for the sake of it. I hoped it would get better as time went on, but it did not seem to be happening. I still had to come home eventually. It was a weird feeling; I longed to come home and have someone waiting for me who was pleased to see me. He always seemed to want to be alone now, strange how the grass is always greener. He would often say that to me.

I made such an effort to bring me up before he came home. I did not want to spoil another evening. I contemplated going over to meet him coming out, but knew how angry he would be. He would never believe it was because I wanted to see him and be with him. He would think I was checking up on him; I think, truthfully, it was a bit of both. Was it so wrong to want to be with someone you love, whenever you can? There is so little time in life. Maybe if he ever loses me or someone else close that he cares about, he will realise what people and feelings really mean in life. I think he believes he would be happier if he did not care for anyone. I seem to have to keep telling him I do not want to be with him twenty-four hours every day. I wish he wanted me with him, just to live together and spend whatever time we could, enjoying each other. I sometimes feel he enjoys letting other people know I am his and how good I am at things, even making me look better than I am at some aspects of life. I need him to show me that he personally likes things about me, not that I am just for show. I do not mean that in an attractive, good looking sense, but in a measure of success. I want it to be for us, not just for others to see. It is difficult to explain to him sometimes that I do not have to sing my own praises to other people. I just need to be happy about myself. He feels I let him down if I do not boast about my success at work. It is just not me when I try.

I wish there could be a magic cure to dispel my doubts. When feeling low, I would think I am never going to conquer this totally. When feeling better, I would think how stupid I had been and say to myself, I will not let it happen again. But when it does and I do not know what has caused it, I wonder if I am stupid not to check for myself. I certainly wished I had checked more things out in the past. Perhaps I could have prevented a lot of it happening. Maybe I should force myself next time I feel that way and say to myself there is no going back – go and do it. I would end up feeling bad either way. If there is nothing to check I will feel guilty and if there is, well, it is the end.

When he came home, I asked too many questions and he got annoyed. I tried not too but I had to ask – stupid things like which pub he went to. Although he told me I had the feeling he did not want to, and wondered why. Then he got angry and I got upset. Another evening spoilt. We did not bother with the wine. I could not work out if it was my fault or his. I knew if it were mine, I could not do anything about it. Something would not let me stop needing to know.

The next day things appeared better again but I always had the feeling that underneath there was still something coming between us. We had not made love yet and I wondered if it was that. Maybe he was concerned about us as well, but somehow it did not happen and we did not talk about it. I needed him to make me feel like it. I had been trying not to want him physically for so long and I was now afraid or unable, I am not sure which, to relax about it. I was worried I would be dry or not as good as her, and more than that, I felt he was having to force himself to want me in that way. When we were out, he seemed to look as if he fancied nearly every other woman that he looked at who was reasonably attractive and not too old. It was often happening and I felt it was a new way of him trying to undermine me. It certainly knocked my self-confidence. I knew I had to put all these thoughts out of my mind, but it seemed impossible when I could see and feel this wedge between us. I just felt he was still clinging onto the relationship with her in some way, thinking about it and comparing her to me. Perhaps he was still in the process of seeing her and breaking it off gently; I still did not totally believe him that he had not seen her again. I would ask myself if I was going round the bend thinking things like that when he had said it was all over. Then I would say I suppose it is only natural to feel insecure and untrusting. No one else would still be together if this happened, but then some other woman may just accept it. They could not think much of themselves if they did, I thought, but maybe they did it for their children. I said to myself, you cannot keep on like this spoiling everything if there is no reason. I decided to try harder to believe him, but did not quite know how I would do it. I still had not spoken to anyone about it or told anyone what I had been through. I felt maybe we needed a holiday together so we could relax. We decided to go away for Easter. I hoped that would be long enough, and hoped he wanted it as well. Maybe he would still prefer to go on his own, that really hurt but he had not mentioned it again.

Chapter 15
Mind Games

I remember the day I asked him if he thought my stomach was swollen. Of course not, he said, with hardly a glance. I would have understood if I had been a hypochondriac, but I was the opposite and it had taken a lot of courage to even ask him. I had not felt right for ages and my stomach ached and, to me, looked swollen most of the time. I thought maybe I caught something all those years ago and it was now coming out, as the doctor had said it might. I thought I probably have a terminal illness and he will finally be rid of me and can have whoever he wants. I thought, I hope it makes him happy, but I do not think it will. I thought if it does not matter to him why should I concern myself? I convinced myself some days it did not matter, but other days it did. Some days I noticed it, others I did not. Some days it felt uncomfortable, not painful, others it did not. When he was not there it seemed to matter more, when he was it did not come into my mind so much. Why he did not see or know or help me, I do not know. Maybe I was glad he did not notice; I believed it would just go away. Faith could sometimes do that.

Things did improve, quite a lot sometimes. We started making love again; it was lovely, not perfect but that was to be expected I suppose. I felt so much better, physically, and mentally. Then something would happen and make me low. I did not know what, maybe just thoughts. All that had happened and been said would go through my mind. I would feel very unsure about his feelings for me. I would wonder if all the things he had said he felt about freedom and being tied, were still in him and he was just covering them up. I seemed to think more about it when he seemed low and distant. This stopped me helping him to get up again as I used to.

Every time he appeared low, I was afraid he was pining for it all again. I knew he had a new job and it was difficult and stressful for him. I wanted to help him so much, more than I could express in words. All I seemed to be doing was asking him questions, which made matters worse. I was unsure and insecure about us – would it last? He appeared so low some days and I had to pretend to be bright when I could to try and help him get up, but he did not seem to want my help. I think he thought it was interference. This made me believe even more that there could still be something going on at lunchtimes, maybe, or the odd evening he stayed at work late. Deep down I did not believe he would do that but then I would say to myself, that is how you felt and what you believed before it all happened. I wanted to tell him how I felt and occasionally I tried, but it never came out very well and seemed to lead to him getting annoyed, or an argument about what I had said or not said. He often repeated what I had said but with a different interpretation of my words. It would make me so angry and frustrated when he did that. Sometimes I just wanted to lash out at anything and hurt him as I was being hurt. As usual, I would control and suppress most of it. The little I did not suppress caused enough problems.

If only he could understand my feelings, perhaps he thought that of me. I still could not understand why he did not want my concern, or want me to share his problems and worries. He gets so annoyed when I try to help. I probably do it in the wrong way, but I do not know what he wants from me in that respect. I cannot pretend I am not interested and do not care, when I do.

Hopefully, our Easter holiday will give us a week to relax and unwind, and perhaps undo some of the harm and repair some of the wounds. I am not silly enough to think the scars will disappear, but some scars can be used positively. I do love him so much, none of that has gone away. In fact, despite it all, I still love him a bit more each day, if that is possible. I think I wanted to stay together more for him than for myself. Next week we will have been married twenty years. I remember the love I felt when we first met, when we were engaged, when we were married. It had always been great and full and unbearably bursting. Also, it has never stopped growing. I hope it never does, but the longer it grows and strengthens the more it hurts when it is injured.

I suppose I really want, or need, him to tell me the things he said about his wants and needs have changed. I do not want him to tell me anything that is not true, but I do want him to feel the way he used to about me and let me know. It will be no good if I tell him what I want to hear from him and he just gives it to me. I think he knows that anyway, but if it is not true, I suppose he does not want to tell me lies. He says words do not mean a lot, it is actions that count. I think it is both. I know words can be said that you really do not mean, especially in anger. We have both said many. The trouble is I do not know the reasons for some of his actions without words to go with them. He comes home early now, sometimes, and I am pleased and know he is doing it for me. I hate it when he is out and I am not sure who he is with, mistrust I suppose. He also sometimes makes me feel he is coming home early but does not want to. I need some words to show me he does want to, if that is the case. I cannot explain the way I feel to him over things like that. He would only deny it if I told him. Maybe it would be true, but how can I know – time I suppose? Perhaps in time he will want to share more with me again. Just thinking about the possibility brings tears to my eyes; I seem very emotional lately. More than I used to be, or perhaps I am finding it harder to cover things up. Perhaps it is just insecurity and worry. I must try harder to overcome it. I really do not want to put more pressure on him now. I certainly do not want to punish him. I just want us back. They say you cannot have the past back – that is not what I want. It is our current and future I want us to have together, in strength with love and confidence. I really do want us to grow old together, take care of each other, love each other, make each other angry, make each other laugh. The laughter is still missing – we must get it back.

It was like a recurring torture. I must get the trust back for my sake as much as his and ours. One could not survive these feelings. At work it would seem fine, I would feel on top again, and then, mostly when things were relaxed, it would all happen again in my mind. I would hear the words that had been said, feel the hurt that I had felt, want to harm her or myself, never James. I wonder why it felt that way. Then I would think the thoughts have come back as a sign that it is not all over. If I asked him, it would just cause more distress.

Perhaps I now wanted more than he had to give. I did not think that it was a lot. Then I only wanted it if he wanted to give it. I did not want to hint or ask for it. I needed him to tell me how he felt about me, and that the other feelings had gone. I suppose if I was honest, I knew they had not gone away, or he would have told me. He did not want to tell me any more lies, I thought. I did not want to hear any. I also really needed to know that he did not still want all those things. It was really torturing me, and I did not know how to stop it. Only he could do that, and he probably did not realise.

Would I ever recover, would we ever recover as a couple, or would we just cope and survive? I was always proud to be called a survivor. I knew now I wanted more than that – I wanted to be on top. Not financially or physically but personally and mentally, to be myself again inside.

Life had become much better and was easier; I could see and feel him caring again but I also knew he was trying to make me feel that. I did not want him to try and make me feel things, I wanted him to want to. All would feel well again and something stupid would bring me down, put thoughts and reminders and doubts in my mind. I would feel so destructive when I got like that, but just seemed to be unable to do anything to stop it. I think it was the bottling up inside me. James was the only person I could speak to about it, no one else knew.

It is strange how things change. I had made up my mind one hundred percent not to tell him about the phone calls which always seemed to come when he was out. It kept trying to come out, I would give hints, then one night after a few drinks I told him. I did not tell him all she said. It was odd he did not show much reaction, it was as if he knew. I told him I had not said anything because I knew that was what she wanted me to do, or guessed I would do. I wonder what she expected from him in response, maybe just contact if there had not been any. Maybe just to hurt me and cause trouble between us. I was glad I had not told him before, but somehow so relieved that I had now. I did not tell him exactly what she said, I could not remember precisely, and I had hung up on them quickly and not said anything. I said I would tell him if it happened again. I hoped it would not as I had become so reluctant to pick up the phone when I was on my own, stupid really but I think I was wanting to say something back, but had made up my mind not to even reply to her. Telling him seemed to lift me for a while and I thought perhaps I just needed to tell him all my feelings, but knew I could not. Maybe one day. To start with it was just, can I speak to James. Then comments like, he is only back with you because he feels guilty. Then we had great times together and why not let him go. Also, there were some silent ones.

He would see me feeling down and say we all go up and down, it will get better. I agreed but I do not think he realised quite how down I was. I did not want him to see. When I was up it did not seem so bad, my insides did not hurt so much, did not feel so suppressed, especially when he would cuddle me. Odd how I longed to be cuddled and stroked, not so much sexually, just to be held and feel close.

The holiday was good for us, but it was not long enough to release all the tension. I think we were just relaxing when we had to come back. The love making was good, but I still knew something was missing on my side and his. I did not know what to do about my feelings. I wanted to love so much; I think too much. It seemed to take ages for me to get aroused and wet, although inside I could not wait. Then sometimes thoughts of him doing this to her made me turn off, and I had to cover it up and pretend. I thought that was best. I could not tell him because the last thing I wanted was for him to feel guilty and know it affected me in that way. I thought, with time it would stop, and I would forget a bit and relax more. What puts thoughts of the past into one's mind – the bad things always come more often than the good? Perhaps you need to force yourself to remember the good. I wish it worked the other way. I must make the effort to recall the wonderful things we have and have done, and maybe there will not be room for the ones I would like to forget.

Chapter 16
I Wish I Knew How

What is it? What is still wrong? I believe he stills loves me. I know he tries to make me feel loved, but it is not working. I feel so insecure. I seem to want him to do everything with me, but I do not say because he never wanted to be like that. I force myself not to tell him, but sometimes the longing in me is so great it seems to break me apart. I think I am always getting on his nerves. I see him wanting to get rid of me. I even sometimes feel the same; I want him not to be there so I can relax. As soon as he is away, I feel awful and want nothing more than to be with him, however horrible it is. I do not mean horrible in the nasty sense just that it is not right between us. I wish I knew how to relax. I think that is part of the problem. I seem to need to be doing something all the time. No wonder I am so tired. I want to do many things, but I end up wasting so much time doing nothing with him and not enjoying it. How do we enjoy each other again? I know we can, but I need to unwind – I wish I knew how. I seem to have tried everything. I long for him just to hold me, that is when I feel okay, but he only does that for a few seconds and then goes away onto other things. I need to be held for hours, not seconds or minutes. Maybe I want and need too much.

There always seems to be pressure on me, perhaps I bring it on myself. I need the shopping and washing and ironing and things to be done before I can relax. He would relax first and do them after, or maybe never. Perhaps he just wants me to do everything because he knows what I am like. I am still trying to carry out my job properly, which is always stressful. Please let our strength together help us to find the way to be in each other's company with pleasure and laughter together again. I feel a part of me is missing since everything happened and it has not yet been repaired or replaced. It seems that when I feel brighter, thoughts of the past come and drag me into the pits again. I dreamt last night of the things that happened over six years ago, when he used to leave for work on a Sunday night instead of Monday morning to be with another woman before this latest one. I had believed he had to work so hard and make an early start on Monday, instead he went to fuck her and be with her. I suppose that is why I felt so low today, but I could not tell him why. I felt like it all happened yesterday but if I told him, he would not understand. He would think I was trying to make him feel guilty.

I feel I am being punished in my life for a crime I do not know I have committed. It sounds weak when you think of the people worse off than you and the suffering in the world, but it does not undo the feelings I have of paying for something I have not done. Stop being so pathetic and feeling sorry for yourself, I say, you do not know how well off you are. Perhaps I should say it more often and it might have some effect, eventually. I need something so badly and I do not know exactly what it is. I know it can only come from James if I ever find it again. I love him too much. There is so much love in me to give, and these feelings are stopping me giving it. How can I overcome them, where are the answers?

What does love mean to you, I said one day. I only love

you and my brother, he said. I asked again, but what does it mean to you. Someone you would hurt yourself for, he replied. Is that all, I asked. He said, yes but I would have to consider to what degree.

I did not say any more. I had never thought of love like that, although I remember when I would have died to save him as I would if I had children that I loved. I did know he had hurt me more than I could ever have imagined, both physically and mentally. I still wanted and loved him but not at any price. I was willing to give it this last try.

Forgive and forget they say. My love was strong enough to forgive, but I do not think it possible I could ever forget. I would love to.

PART FOUR
LATER

Chapter 17
Abroad

We did get closer again, slowly, but there was what seemed like a brick or glass wall between us, stopping us getting as close as we needed, preventing us putting the past behind us. I found it impossible to fully trust him, unable to believe I was not deceiving myself and that he was not lying to me. I wondered if I had made a big mistake having him back. Then he came home one day and told me he had been offered a secondment in Europe for at least a year, and maybe longer. I was devastated, but as usual told him how pleased I was for him. Life had been difficult enough with all my concerns when he was working away and not home for the odd night. It was impossible to trust him, although I wanted to. How could I cope with this new development? It was a great opportunity and he really wanted to take the job, but seemed to show some worry about me. He said I would be allowed to go with him and perhaps that would help to put the past behind us. He was basically suggesting I give up my job which I had worked so hard at to get, as if it did not matter at all. He said we could be comfortable on his salary and he would earn a lot more. I knew I would be giving up a great deal and if it did not work out, I would be financially unable to support myself. One thing I was determined about after what I had been through nearly losing the house, was that I would always stay financially independent. He suggested I ask for a year off, like maternity leave. That really hurt but I said nothing. He seemed to think I wanted to stop him going, and his old behaviour came back with words about being tied twenty-four hours a day to me. All I had done was say I was reluctant to give up my job. I needed time to think about it, but he said he had to decide and let them know otherwise the job would go to someone else.

I thought about it a lot on my own and decided I would encourage him one hundred percent to go for it. I also felt if I had some time without him, the ball was on the other foot – I might be able to be my old confident and positive self. I would be living a single life in England while he was working in Europe. If I found out he did the same again, then I knew I would have the strength to live without him on my own. I would not let him hurt me that much again despite my love for him. It was hard, but I put on a positive face and gave him an encouraging response and supported him fully, telling him how much I wanted him to succeed.

He got the job and we packed together, I dropped him off at the airport and he went off with a contract for three years.

As I drove home it was as if he had left me again, and all the hurt and words that had been said came back in my heart, in my head and my body. I went home and sobbed until there was nothing left, but I was determined to be strong and look after myself and get me back again. I was really a very self-confident and self- sufficient lady. My weakness was my love for James. I had let it destroy me, instead of how it used to be my strength.

Those first few weeks, he called me regularly, seemed to miss me. He was struggling with the job and said he was not sure he had done the right thing. He did not like his female boss; he had never had one before. I knew what that was like as I had males working under me and it could be difficult. I encouraged him to keep at it, not to give up and appear a failure. He found an apartment to rent which sounded genuinely nice. I thought, he still owns a flat here in England, but we did not mention that. He had let it out to a colleague's son and the rental income was paying the mortgage. I did not want anything to do with the place, but he seemed to think I would manage things if necessary while he was away.

He did start to like the job after a few months and learnt that he would have to travel to many other countries in the world to fulfil his contract. After about six weeks he asked me to visit him and drive his car over, which he said he needed. I took a couple of days leave and decided to go for a long weekend. I had been coping well on my own. It was a kind of relief knowing where he was, even though not with me. I did not have to cope with his up and down moods in the evenings and over the weekends, which had left me with feelings of inadequacy. I did not realise how much they had been affecting me until I felt better about myself. I said to myself, absence makes the heart grow fonder. I wonder if that will be true for either or both of us.

I visited him and helped him set up comfortably in his apartment, and delivered his car. He took me out and about and showed me the town and his office, and we made love. It was different this time, I did not do it thinking of him making love to someone else and I really enjoyed it again. There was still the past between us, but I felt he had missed me and that the love was still there. He was still struggling a bit with the job and his boss, but he had decided to persevere and was getting into a life with his colleagues, he said. I wondered about the women in the office, but I put it to the back of my mind. I must learn to trust again. Effectively, he had the life he told me he had craved, free to do what he wanted, thinking of his needs and wants. He never thought about me having the same. I was living the life of a single woman working with powerful men. I was still attractive. I do not know if he gave that any thought. He did not even ask me about what I did in the evenings or weekends, or show any interest in my work. It was all about him.

It was extremely difficult leaving; I wanted to stay with him. I put on a brave face as usual. He said I could visit again whenever I wanted, and maybe I could accompany him on some of his foreign trips, maybe China and Africa. He had to visit many places across the world. I would really love to visit all these places. I had always wanted to travel, but never had the opportunity or money. But I had my career and job, and was determined to stay financially independent because I knew if he ever did it to me again, we would separate and I would need to buy him out of the house. On the way home I decided I would have to organise my own life a bit better. I needed to plan what I would do apart from my work.

It was difficult and complicated. I used to be a very sociable person, we had joint friends and separate friends, but we had done most things as a couple. At work it was no problem, I was always on my own socially, but everyone knew I was married. As male colleagues learnt that James was working away, moves were made to ask me to join social things outside work. I was an attractive lady. I told lies – I said, I am busy with friends or family, and avoided it all. Instead I went home, and I isolated myself without realising. I would work at home in the evenings, sometimes at weekends as well.

If my family asked me over, I would say I was working. My sole leisure was a swim and a sauna on Saturday morning, this I did alone. All the work I put in had a reward as I was promoted at work myself. James seemed pleased when I told him, but not overjoyed. I worked in a male environment and mixed with powerful and attractive men, and was frequently propositioned. I must be honest – I found some attractive and I needed to be treated nicely by a man. However, I stuck to my guns and turned them all down. I could not do the same thing to James that he had to me, however tempting. The thought of hurting him that much if he found out, hurt me all over again. I think I loved him too much, if that is possible.

Basically, I spent no money, except on food, as I did not have much of a life. I saved a lot, but did not tell him in case I needed it. We had always had joint funds but now I had a separate account of my own – I needed it for security.

James had started working with a team of Americans and they came over to London with him for a conference. I was invited as his wife to an evening meal to meet them, along with other English colleagues and their wives. They all seemed a friendly crowd and I enjoyed the evening. I am a very perceptive person and there was one female among the group who made a special effort to meet me, and I saw her weighing me up. I knew immediately she fancied James and would make a play for him. She was married, but her husband was in the States. My thoughts were, would he succumb and how would I know? If he does, that is the end of us. I did not say anything to him as I knew he would criticise me for not trusting him. He rarely came home to England, so I did not want to spoil the visit.

I continued to visit him whenever I could take a long

weekend from work, and we always seemed pleased to see each other and were happy together. We had lovely weekends, but this was not the same as being man and wife at home.

James made many trips around the world, often in the company of the Americans and the woman I knew who fancied him. One trip they were all flying back via London, so I went to pick him up at the airport. The husband of the American woman was also waiting to pick her up. She came out before James and I saw her look at her husband; it was clear they were not a happy couple although they greeted each other in a friendly manner. She then saw me and said hello and gave me a look. Only some women would know but it showed a kind of jealousy, or 'I could have had him' look. I was not sure which, but it made all the distrust and insecurities surface. James arrived about ten minutes later and I had managed to perk up again. I had been so looking forward to seeing him. We hugged and kissed, and my heart swelled with love. I felt like crying. He seemed so pleased to see me. I saw him and her have a look between them. We did not get introduced to her husband. I thought if there is something going on with her, I will know. Was I just being suspicious because of the past and my insecurity and lack of trust? We went home; he was very loving towards me and told me all about the trip. I asked about the other people. He said they were typical Americans – hard-working but a bit gung-ho and always thought they were right. He said he got along with them okay. I asked about the woman in the context that she was in the same position as me, a lone woman working with all men. He said she just fitted in, went running with the men and was good at her job. He said they had gone to the swimming pool together and she was a bit of a bean pole. I said no more; I did not want to ask if she had tried it on with him, but I knew she had. I could not be sure he had said no but I hoped.

I later learnt that she had split up with her husband and had an affair with one of the American men on the team, and was now living with another who had left his wife. I was right about her and hoped James had turned her down, which would have accounted for the look she gave me.

The job for James continued well for the year, and they confirmed the extension of the contract for a further two years. I had managed to build myself up and progress my career, but I stayed lonely. My social life was visiting James' mother and my own on a regular basis. They were both widowed and getting older. I cut myself off from old friends and my job became my life.

James and I spoke on the phone regularly and we never mentioned the past. He was enjoying his job and his freedom, I could tell. I received a few postcards from him when he was travelling. He always said he missed and loved me. I felt I was giving up my life for him. I was in my forties, still attractive, no children, still having physical needs but no life apart from the odd weekend together. I used my annual leave to make some of the visits longer, and we did grow close again when together.

On my side, there was still always something missing. I wanted him to regret what he had done. I did not want to ask. I wanted to know he never really loved the others, although at the time he said he did. I wanted, and needed, him to tell me. I had trusted him too much and I always believed he loved me too much to cheat on me. I had one hundred and ten percent confidence in it when I was at my happiest all those years ago. I realised I had become a sad person and my personality had changed. I was no longer full of mischief and fun, willing to have a go at anything. Where had I gone? I worked hard. I thought a lot, but socially my interpersonal skills had disappeared. I felt I was waiting for him to come home for me to get me back again. That would never work – I had to get back to being myself by myself.

I tried. I put more into work and was promoted again, against all expectations. I had a big staff and a pressure job, and I was good at it. I mixed a bit more socially at work, and made friends with some of my male and female colleagues. I would go to the pub and out for meals, but always in a group. I did get taken to the odd business lunch sometimes by men and I always enjoyed it. Some touched on my husband being away and asked me out, but I always turned them down, despite occasionally being attracted to, and tempted by, the person. It gave me a bit of my old self confidence back, but I knew I could never have that 'nothing can knock me down' confidence again. I also knew I would never let anyone make me so low again. I made friends at the gym where I went swimming, and I started a course of French lessons. I put a lot into my small garden and became friends with some of the neighbours. I did not feel quite so isolated, but it was an unnatural and uncomfortable way of life. However, I persevered. The time arrived when the end of the contract for James was due.

He told me he would have the option of a further contract or going back to his old post. I was in a turmoil. If he came back, how would we be? Would he be in contact with her again? Had he been in contact with her while he was away? I should not think of all these things, but they just came into the mind. What if he takes another contract and continues to be away? Have I got to carry on with this sad, lonely life, pretending to family and people around me that I am happy and busy, with a big social life? I knew I had been doing this.

I decided I would say the decision was up to him. I wanted him home but not as it was when he left. I wanted him to be happy with his work and with me. I would not ask or tell him what I wanted, that was my decision. I was concerned either way. I thought if he came home it would be make or break. Up till now our marriage had survived and I believed our love as well, but maybe I was kidding myself and had just been hanging out the inevitable break up.

The uncertainty lasted several months, exceedingly difficult times for me. Then a third option was put on the table. He could opt for early retirement, and take his pension early with a lump sum. I thought, he is too young to retire, but he could take the money and find another job if he wanted. I did not say anything to influence his decision, apart from it was his choice and I would support him with it. I waited for him to say what he had decided.

While he was away, the people renting his flat had moved out so there had been no income from it for a while. He seemed to think I should have found another tenant, but I wanted nothing to do with it, so I just left it. It still hurt too much to even go inside it. I was afraid if he came back he might want to move back into it, so I asked if he wanted to let it short term to some friends of mine who were in between buying and selling a house. He agreed to this so when he came over for a visit, we went together to look at the flat. The people who had rented it had left it as a tip. He was angry at me that I had not been and sorted it out. I tried to explain that to me it was his not mine, he said we had bought it in joint names. It bought back the past again. I agreed to help him clean it up and replace what was necessary to let it again. I also suggested selling it. He gave me a funny look and did not respond. I thought, he is keeping his options open to maybe move in again himself. How could I be such a fool, I thought, as to think it is all behind us.

Was this the end or was there a future for us? Had he any idea what my life had been like for the last three years, and how I had lived? I doubted it. Would it go back to where it left off if he came back? Was she, or other women, out of the picture? I had built myself into someone different. I would not let it destroy me again.

I had been sad, lonely and frustrated, and sorely tempted to have a relationship while he was away. I really liked some of the men who tempted me. Lust, at a certain time in one's life, can be mistaken for love, but it does not last. I just knew I did not love them. I was still, after all that had happened, in love with James.

Had I wasted opportunities for love over those years? I had plenty of offers and temptations. I was crying out inside to be loved. My problem was, I was still in love with James. I had tried not to be, tried to fancy other guys. To be honest, I did fancy some of them and was tempted but it would just have been sex or lust, not love. I could not make myself want that. To me I was still married, still too much in love with my husband and I did not want someone else. I knew other ladies who just wanted to see if they had missed anything. They said sex could be quite different with other blokes. It was just not me. I was just too faithful during that period.

Chapter 18
Retirement

Decision made – no new contract. He came home and went back to his old job for six months to train his successor, after which it was agreed he would take early retirement.

It was not an easy six months; we had both got used to living alone, doing our own thing, not saying whether you would be home for dinner. If he said he was having a drink after work with mates, I would be suspicious. It was hard to trust him, but I wanted to. I had waited three years to see if our marriage would survive. I think I was still very insecure but desperate for us to be happy and relaxed together and when we were apart.

He retired and had the opportunity of a consultancy back in Europe, which he decided to turn down. He said he did not think it would be good for us. It was the first time I thought, he wants there to be a normal us, he has said he is doing something because of us. However, he was suddenly at home all day while I still had a demanding job. For the first time, I wanted to give up my career for him so we could be together. I could not afford to just give up my pension rights and have no income. I still needed to be financially secure in my own right. I remembered when he left all that time ago now, and he had tried to get me to agree to sell the house and put the money in the joint bank account until we had both found somewhere new to buy. At that time, I had not trusted him not to walk off with all the money. He was not the man I loved and trusted at that time. It could happen again.

He really seemed to try hard. The first day I came home from work he had cooked me a meal. This was the first time ever, other than the occasional omelette. I just burst into tears. He cooked most days after that, did the shopping and housework. I loved the fact that he was doing it all for me, but I hated it as well. To me I was the wife and I did not feel like one. I did not know how lucky I was. Although I did really, but I was afraid it would not last. I knew he would get bored and would need something more. He did not seem to have any inclination to find another job.

Our social life was different; we did eat out a lot, go to the cinema and gym. We would meet up with family and old friends, but many had moved from the area. The old routines with friends had been phased out of our lives. We would often go to the pub but only the two of us.

Because our mothers were on their own, the Christmas lunch always fell to me. I had always loved to do it, but now all I could think about was the one when he had left me. Instead of fun and a pleasure, it became a pretentious chore and I could not beat the sadness, despite trying extremely hard. The scars were still quite raw.

Due to budget cuts my company was looking for people to offer for redundancy or early retirement. I thought a lot about it and decided to offer myself. They did not want me to go, I had a key role and was well thought of, so they said no. I was extremely disappointed and decided that was what I now really wanted. James and I could then do something totally different together – all the options were open. We had always been a good team when we wanted. I thought we could both do something new and less stressful, perhaps even our own business. The more I thought, the more I wanted it. I hated James being at home and me working, it did not seem natural. I had to keep stopping myself asking what he was doing, and where he was, during the day. He never seemed to want to say. I was still afraid he would re-contact her and it would all resurface again.

It took a while but eventually, due to financial difficulties in the company, they agreed to restructure and let me go. In my head, I had planned enjoying London, which I always loved and never had enough time to visit all the galleries, museums, and exhibitions. We could do this together. We could spend time in France and travel to all the countries I have never had time to visit. My mind was a whirl of what we would, and could, do together. I had saved a lot, James had earned a lot, so between us with our lump sums we would be quite comfortable. We could always perhaps get part time jobs to supplement our pensions. All the potential was a huge lift to me after so many years of a mundane existence and frustration.

We did not discuss details of what we would do, but just talked generally of the opportunities we would have.

The day came and with elation, no sadness, I retired from a phenomenally successful career. We were both young enough to choose what we did with our future.

We took a holiday and it seemed like before it all happened, well almost because we were no longer poor as we had been in our early days together. There was, and probably always will be, something missing, but I said to myself, maybe we can build something stronger together. Learn and profit from what we have been through. We did not discuss the past very much. I usually brought it up after too many drinks. Then, I was only looking for reassurance and still some sort of regret from James, but he did not seem to have it to give me. I had to be satisfied with what we have now. I never questioned whether I still loved him. I had tried not to but now believed true love could not be destroyed, maybe damaged, but it would always remain.

We just enjoyed being at home after the holiday for a few weeks. James had been home for over a year in the daytime regularly, something I had never done. He had been irritated by some of the neighbours and thought we should think about moving. I loved my house and the situation, so convenient for the theatres and everything in London I loved. I did not say no, but I really did not want to move. I asked where he wanted to move to and what kind of house and I said, anyway, we should sell his flat first. We sold the flat quickly, which was a huge relief to me. Then he said he had done that and now he wanted us to move out of London to the country, and get a big house and a garden. He wanted to be a landowner, be something different. I thought to myself, there are only two of us, no children, we do not need a big house or big garden. I did say this, but he said he just wanted to have a look at what was out there and how much we would get if we sold our house. I agreed there was no harm looking, it might be fun, but it was not what I wanted. Why was I so accommodating? I have managed a team of people for years, been so positive and assertive, known my own mind and yet I just go along with his wants. I suppose he has always been a bit selfish, but love is blind. You only see the strengths not the weaknesses when you are totally, totally in love.

We very easily found a buyer for our house, it was a

sought after gem; we should never have let it go, but we did. That was what James wanted.

Finding something else was not so easy. It was an eye opener what was available in the countryside for the money we had, but I was a Londoner through and through – we both were. I kept thinking this is a mistake. We found houses I liked but not where I liked. He became irritated with me as he seemed to like everything we looked at; he was not discerning enough. I eventually found an area I said I would be happy to look at. We found a house immediately he loved but I did not, but I agreed to make a low offer to keep the peace, thinking they will not accept. They did. I kept thinking maybe it will grow on me, but when we went back with a surveyor, I decided I just could not live in it, it was just not me and could never be my home. I thought, this is going to be the end of us, I would have to let him know. If he wants to live here, it will have to be on his own. I had prepared for a separation for a long time. I would have to get on with it; maybe I should have done it years ago, but this was just too much. At least it would not be over another woman. Luck, for a change, was on my side. The surveyor said there were problems with the property, and he could not recommend we purchase it. We went back to the estate agent and withdrew our offer. James was furious because he wanted to sell the London house at the price agreed, and we could lose the purchaser if we did not find somewhere quickly. He tried to get me to agree to sell and rent somewhere while we carried on looking. I stood my ground and would not agree. It was too risky for me. I still did not fully trust him. The agent offered us some other properties to look at in the area, one had just come back on the market because of a chain problem. We had a look, and both liked the house, although I still did not really want to move. The seller said, whichever of you completes first of the two of us who wanted it, could have it. I have to say I secretly hoped it would be the other party. It turned out to be us.

We sold, we moved. There was so much to do; everything needed renovating, decorating, the garden was neglected and huge. There was also so much to learn about country life; we were down a country lane and could not see other houses. We did not know anybody who lived in the area. It was a totally new life together. Would it work?

We made a few friends in our new life, took up new interests, had occasional contact with old friends. James was no longer as sociable as before, certainly not when I was with him. It always sounded as if he had a good time in male company, or when he did things without me. I always felt something was missing when we mixed with other people, but I could not identify what it was. Neither of us found time for a part time job or voluntary work, which had always been in the back of my mind. The house and garden required so much time and effort to improve and maintain, that it became our life. James did not want to travel; he said he had enough of that when he was working. He did not seem to consider that I had not travelled further than Europe, and had wanted to all my life. Instead of doing that, I was putting my retirement into a house I had not wanted, although I had grown to love it and what we had made it into. It became a home for us. It had been good for us, I admitted finally, to move from London where, in the end, I had been so sad. I did resent underneath my façade to everyone I knew that I was young, retired and comfortable, but could not follow my ambitions to see parts of the world I always dreamt of seeing. Like some other ambitions, I accepted it as the price of love. It was my choice, or was it?

After a few years of ups and downs, I really did agree we had made the right decision in moving out of London, and we had a good life. We would travel a lot to Europe, but no further. We were happy together, lucky to be retired so early. We were fit and active, but something was still missing. All our contemporaries of a similar age were becoming grandparents. I did not realise it until it happened, but all the feelings of disappointment of not having children came back. I could not mention it to James for fear of making him feel guilty, and I did not want him to. It was not his fault, just a bit of bad luck in life. So, I kept it to myself. We would mix with people and all they would talk about would be the grandchildren. It was nice to hear but eventually became boring because the old conversation topics died away. I got quite low often when this type of thing arose, and had to fight the sadness off. I learnt long ago never to feel sorry for myself. I did not know what James thought at these times; he never seemed to regret not having children or grandchildren. He never regretted his transgressions. He would only admit to regretting what he did to me. In my heart I knew the two feelings were different. I wanted the regrets that were not there.

Generally, we were happy and lucky compared to the ones whose marriages did not survive. Most I knew regretted the divorce or separation, and wished they had stayed together. The second relationship or marriage hardly ever lasted long term. Both parties often ended up old, sad and lonely, and full of regrets. A few were a success, but in the minority. If I was honest, we had far more happy times than sad ones.

Everybody has strengths and weaknesses. If you love someone you accept both and really get to know both. I tried to draw from his strengths, even copy them. I tried to give support to his weaknesses. He seemed to love it all at first, but somewhere along the line he came to resent my help. Maybe he was not happy if I could do something better than him. He never liked to fail at anything and always liked to win. He could be childish if he did not get his own way, but I accepted this was the person he was that I fell in love with. It changed when he started to get selfish and aggressive. It did not happen overnight, it was a gradual process. I did not realise for a while. I became frustrated at never seeming to do what I wanted, always fitting in with his wants and needs, so I observed him and saw how he manipulated the conversation, or decision making, to steer towards what he wanted and dismiss what I wanted. Minor things to start with as to what to watch on TV, then later the bigger issues like where, or even if, we went on holiday, if we bought a car, who to invite home or who to visit. If we did end up doing what I wanted, he would find a way to spoil it.

I remembered him telling me when he was looking at coming back to me, that he had carried out a SWOT analysis. I think I was too much in shock at the time and so low I did not give it enough thought. Maybe I should have done one as to whether to have him back. Strengths and weaknesses must have been easy as we knew each other so well. Opportunities or threats, I cannot imagine what was on his list. I should have wondered what characteristic in a person would do that analysis to decide whether to keep their marriage together. Maybe he should do one now because he is pushing me away. Then, the other side of him appears and he tells me how much he loves me, how we are joined together, how I am his right arm. I do not want us to part, I never have, but I do not want these frequent bursts of hostility towards me when he does not get his own way, or does not agree with my opinion on something. Is this the price I will have to pay for love in my old age?

We had some really bad times. There were phases; he never let me finish a question if I tried to sort it out with him. One day I was so exasperated that I wrote him a note. It said, something terrible is going to happen if these verbal outbursts from you continue. They seem to happen if I do something you do not like or want, or if you are not getting your own way. Also, if I disagree with something you say or want. You will not listen when I tell you. It is spoiling our whole life. It seems if you know I like something, you want to stop it, spoil it, or change it. Why? Yet you say you love me. Can you not enjoy what we have before it is too late, and we do not have each other any longer?

I did not need him to do things for me to make it right. I just wanted him to stop being like that to me. Generally, I was a happy person, but he could make me so sad and unhappy.

I tried to make myself be like him, be a bit selfish and only go for what I wanted, but it never lasted because it was just not me. I still cared too much about his happiness and well-being. If I behaved like him, I was not happy with myself.

When he was in one of his discontented phases, I told him to leave me and go and be happy elsewhere without me. I even suggested, after all these years, he was still pining for one of his other women. The scars were obviously still there. After times like this he would say, everything will be okay because we love each other. I would try again, waiting for his next nasty phase. I tried all sorts – ignoring, humouring, saying nothing, but always ended up pointing out what he was doing to me before he would stop. He often blamed me for making him like it, but never identified what I was supposed to have done.

I learnt that these phases would pass, but sometimes I felt like just going away and that I had made a big mistake letting him stay in my life.

I often thought about these women who knowingly have a relationship with a married man. Do they know what damage they can cause short and long term? Do they really want to keep a man that does that to his wife who he loved or still loves? He will do it to them as well. That is why, at the time, I had to know all I could learn about them once I knew of them. Maybe there were others I never heard about or noticed. These thoughts still came into my mind when I felt unloved.

Chapter 19
Growing Old, Any Regrets

We were lucky we had retired early, had a lovely home. We were not rich but wonderfully comfortable. We still had our little get away property in France, albeit a bit rough and dilapidated.

We grew close again. I knew it would never be the same as it was before, but I also knew our love had never gone away and the decision to stay together had been the right one. I did not have regrets. I had not loved anyone else I met enough to want to be their wife. It was only at the sad, difficult moments that I thought I should have refused to have him back all those years ago. I knew I had never wanted a life without him, but there was a limit to the price I would pay in the hurt department. There was a big scar inside which would never go away. But, like any scar, it fades over the years and just occasionally surfaces as a problem when touched or knocked in the wrong way.

We took up new activities, things we had never had the time or money for. We even learnt to ski in our old age, which produced a lot of fun and happiness for us both.

There were things I would have liked to do, places I would have liked to travel to and see, but James did not. I wanted him to be contented but I often felt I was being frustrated in my old age. I felt my hands were tied behind my back, or I had a ball and chain which made it difficult to achieve my desires. I could not identify anywhere he really wanted to travel to. I had a long list with not much ticked off, and I started to feel I had left it too late for many of the places were no longer attractive as the world had changed so much. He said he was content to stay in England.

I often sensed James' discontentment, despite having so much and now being mostly where he wanted to be. I often wondered if it was not having children, and then grandchildren, but I never raised that subject. I learnt, although it took a long time, that he would strive hard for what he wanted until he got it. He very soon became bored with what he had achieved and would want something different. He lost sight of what we had sometimes and how privileged we had become. It was rare I could say I saw him happy and contented. If I asked if he was happy, he would just say, what does that mean? For a long time, I was never one hundred percent sure he was glad we were together; would he have preferred that single life he used to crave, or to be with someone else?

Our love for each other was strong. I always knew that to be true, but he never reassured me. He would tell me he loved me and that I was his right arm, but I always felt there was a 'but' underneath those words. He had once said love is a disease or illness, like a virus.

We gradually grew older together and we both had some health issues. When James had problems, I was extremely supportive and luckily all was resolved. As you reach a certain age you start to hear of people not surviving illnesses, or ending up with no quality of life so, again, we had been lucky.

Then it was my turn and I could not believe how well James looked after me. He seemed desperate not to lose me and for me to recover quickly.

It was then he told me things I had waited so long to hear. I think perhaps he had seen me as strong and capable of overcoming all the past hurt. He did not see my vulnerability or the need to reassure me until I had health problems. I knew the past could not be undone, but I had wanted for so long to know.

One day he told me he had never ever loved anyone else. He had just wanted to try a different way of life, but had realised how much he loved me and had made his choice at the time. He said he never ever did not love me, he just wanted other things and I would not let him have them as well as me, so he had made his decision and here he is. It was as if a huge burden or cancerous growth had been taken away. I could not remember when I felt so at peace.

He said to me, if only you knew how much you are loved, you would be incredibly happy.

He said to me, you could have done a lot better than me. I know I held you back and stopped you reaching your full potential, doing things you wanted to do. You should have married someone like a solicitor or accountant. I said, not me, there was never anyone else for me. I am, and always will be, a one-man woman.

He would tell other people I was his right hand. We were growing old happily together. Luckily again my health issues were resolved and together we have celebrated our golden wedding. He tells me a lot that he loves me, and I believe it now. I feel loved as well, how lucky I am not to have let it go.

I have no regrets; who knows how much longer we will have together. We still have each other. I was sometimes sad at having no children and grandchildren, but we had so much together it did not matter in the same way now as it had all those years ago when I suppressed all those feelings. The price I had paid, maybe we had paid, was worth it. Despite all the sad and bad times, we had a great marriage with loads of love and happiness. We had grown stronger in many ways. I knew he would be there to support me when I needed him, even if he had become a selfish and grumpy old man. I was confident of his love for me and mine for him, I had never doubted.

I do not think either of us would be happy with ourselves if we had gone our separate ways. In the bad times I always knew there was light at the end of the tunnel.

A one-way love can be broken. A two-way love can survive, despite the lapses and indiscretions, if you want it to. The price is worth paying; such love is hard to find and easy to lose. Scars heal quicker with love. If you have true love, fight for it, and keep it.

Some people go a lifetime and are never loved or love; how lucky we had been, even if we did not both recognise it at the time. Life may have been boring if it had all run smoothly.

Happiness and hurt, love and betrayal, that is life, get on with it. Never, ever feel sorry for yourself. Do not give up on love. True love is worth whatever price you pay to keep it. It is special.

When I look back now, there was an awful lot of pain but there was a lot more love in my life over the years. Eventually it is the good that wins and the bad fades.

Chapter 20
Now

Later I wrote this poem.
Love arrives
And then it dies
An ecstasy that can break the heart
Though you never want to be apart
It may last an hour of lust
Then disappear like a cloud of dust
It may even last a week
To find it is not what we seek
Maybe a month will pass
Before it shatters like glass
It may even be one-sided
When the two hearts become divided
It can run on for years
Then end with many tears
Even last for decades
To finish when one side fades
But when it lasts for a lifetime
Like a learnt and treasured rhyme
It is something extra special
As if someone cast a spell
Which kept two hearts together
To grow just like wild heather
But sadly, that will die
When life ends and we say goodbye